BY THE SAME AUTHOR

Non Fiction

A Just Measure of Pain, the Penitentiary in the Industrial Revolution, 1750–1850

Wealth and Virtue: The Shaping of Classical Political Economy in the Scottish Enlightenment (co-edited, with Istvan Hont)

The Needs of Strangers

The Russian Album

Fiction

Asya

SCAR TISSUE

MICHAEL IGNATIEFF

VIKING
Published by the Penguin Group
Penguin Books Canada Ltd, 10 Alcorn Avenue,
Toronto, Ontario, Canada M4V 3B2
Penguin Books Ltd, 27 Wrights Lane, London W8 5TZ, England
Viking Penguin, a division of Penguin Books USA Inc.,
375 Hudson Street, New York, New York 10014, U.S.A.
Penguin Books Australia Ltd, Ringwood, Victoria, Australia
Penguin Books (NZ) Ltd, 182-190 Wairau Road,
Auckland 10, New Zealand

Penguin Books Ltd, Registered Offices:
Harmondsworth, Middlesex, England

First published 1993

1 3 5 7 9 10 8 6 4 2

Publisher's note: This book is a work of fiction. Names, characters, places and incidents either are the product of the author's imagination or are used fictitiously, and any resemblance to actual persons living or dead, events, or locales is entirely coincidental.

Printed and bound in Canada on acid free paper

Canadian Cataloguing in Publication Data

Ignatieff, Michael
Scar tissue

ISBN 0-670-85048-9

I. Title.

PS8567.G63S33 1993 C813'.54 C93-093822-4
PR9199.3.I56S33 1993

For A. G. I.
For J. A. G. I.

So by this infirmity may I be perfected, by
this completed. So in this darkness,
may I be clothed in light.

I DO NOT WANT to remember her last hour. I do not want to be eternally condemned to think of her as she was in those final moments, when we held her hands, my brother and I, and she fought for life and lost, her mouth stretched open, gasping for breath, her eyes staring sightlessly up into the lights. That scene goes on and on, as if it will never end, as if some unreconciled part of me still denies that it actually occurred. I still have days when everything she ever was, everything she ever meant to me is entirely erased by the memory of those great agonising breaths, that frail body wracked with spasms, those lips wet with blood. There must be some way to redeem this, some way to believe that the banal heartlessness of it all was not for nothing. There must be some way back to the unscarred beginnings, when she was in her painting clothes, barefoot, sipping a beer, humming to herself, happy and far away. That is how she should be remembered. That is what I must rescue from her dying, if such a thing can be done.

How do I tell her story? When does it actually begin? When does that dying begin? It was within her from the beginning, an illness passed from cell to cell, from mother to daughter. In my brother's lab I have seen those cells, the dark starbursts of scar tissue, invisible to the naked eye. I have seen the inheritance, the family silver.

Which of the ancestors was the first to feel it coming? I cannot be sure. The thing was called different names then, if it was called an illness at all. Only now can we begin to give it a name. The family legend is that Annie MacDonald had it, though she didn't know herself.

She was born in Scotland in the middle of the last century and came out here in the 1870s. She met a country schoolmaster, became his wife and brought three children into the world. Pictures survive of her husband and her children, but not of Annie MacDonald.

I do not need pictures. I see her plainly enough. She is walking along a rutted country road, between stump-filled fields, her bonnet tied round her chin, her crinolines dragging in the dirt. Farmers in the fields stop to watch her pass. She is heading in the direction of the setting sun, and she passes all the lighted windows in the clearings until there is nothing but woods on either side. Deep in the forest, she stumbles and falls. A boy heading home in a cart finds her there. Her bonnet lies beside her on the pine needles, and her kerchief is knotted in her fist. When he dismounts and comes over to take a closer look, she stares up at him with empty eyes.

We had few secrets as a family, but we had silences, and this was one of them. Annie MacDonald was my great-grandmother but I never heard a word about her until my brother mentioned, in an offhand way, what she died of – as if I already knew.

Annie MacDonald had three daughters. One of them was called Nettie. She was my mother's mother. As a child I spent nearly every Sunday with her in her apartment on the second floor of an old frame house in the city.

My memory of that apartment is bleached and faded. Rooms have disappeared, a staircase spirals upwards into nothingness in my mind. I do remember a Turkish carpet which stretched down the long dark hall to the kitchen, a carved wooden chest in the hallway; a dusty bookcase in the study and some worn easy chairs round the fireplace in the sitting room. Watery light streamed through the plants she grew in Atlas battery jars on her window sills.

She stayed in bed on Sunday mornings and, if I was staying overnight, we would have tea and buttered biscuits from a tray on her lap in her bedroom. She would read *The Times* of London, a week late, in the lightweight international edition that felt like ash between your fingers; and as she scanned the paper she would ask me what I thought about the headlines. I see myself standing by her bed in pyjamas and slippers, about eight years old, talking nonsense in a high voice. Nettie is propped up on her pillows, listening with a sardonic expression, her long grey and black hair combed out on her nightdress. Then she reaches over to her night table and picks up a jagged piece of dirty crimson silk in a glass frame.

When she asks me whether I know its story, I shake my head, though I know it by heart. She was in England in 1916 and her husband was serving with a regiment in France. During his absence a young soldier from a nearby barracks used to come to have tea with her. He was waiting to be sent up to the trenches. He sat in Nettie's parlour and she talked and he listened not saying a word, his teacup resting on the knee of his uniform.

The next time he came back, on leave from the trenches, he brought her the piece of crimson silk. It had been part of the vestments on the statue of a saint in a French church, and he had crawled into the rubble-filled nave to get it for her. He then went back to the front and never returned. She had the scrap of silk framed to remember him by. 'He was so shy he could hardly enter the room,' is all that I remember her saying about him.

I want to remain faithful to Nettie, to the tortoiseshell comb in her hair, her small, strong hands, her grey eyes. I want to commemorate the attention she paid to me and to a lonely and frightened soldier. I want to hold her in my mind's eye as clearly as I see the wine-coloured lilac bush in the street below my apartment. Memory is the only afterlife I have ever believed in. But the forgetting inside us cannot be stopped. We are programmed to betray.

A year or so later, Nettie is in the front hall of her apartment, holding the crimson silk in her hand. My mother has come to pick me up at the end of the weekend, and we are trying to say goodbye and leave.

'Do you know the story?' Nettie begins.

We both nod. Nettie looks up into our faces.

'It's alright, Nettie, I know the story,' my mother says.

'I want to . . . '

I am making for the door and the long stairway down to the street. Mother signals for me to stay where I am.

'Tell us, Nettie.'

Nettie looks at the crimson fragment, wishing it could speak, and then she looks at me, framed in the doorway, wanting to go, with my mother's hand on my sleeve keeping me there.

So it is Mother who tells the story, looking straight into Nettie's eyes. At the end, she kisses her and we escape, me running down the stairs as fast as my legs will carry me.

A few months later, the police phoned my mother and said they had caught up with Nettie near the K Mart, striding along the road, about a half a mile from home, with her black-and-grey hair falling down about the collar of her housecoat. The policeman got out of his car and touched her arm and asked her name, she couldn't say who she was. When Mother and I got to the police station, Nettie was sitting on a bench beside a policewoman who was drinking coffee from a styrofoam cup and holding

Nettie's hand. Nettie's pink housecoat was the same. Her slippers were the same. Yet when she raised her eyes to meet mine, she didn't have the faintest idea who I was.

I can remember feeling as cold and empty as her vacant eyes. I can remember wondering, even then, why I felt merely distant and curious. This must have been the first time I turned something I at first found fearful into something interesting.

I never went to see her in the institution. I never asked to, either. So it was a surprise when the day came for her funeral. It was as if she had already been dead for years. I remember almost nothing about the ceremony, except that at the very end, one of the men from the funeral home removed a vial from his pocket and poured a thin stream of Nettie's ashes onto the lid of a coffin in the centre of the chapel. When I saw that, I hid my face in my hands.

I've always thought of that moment at Nettie's funeral as the instant my childhood ended. It was as if I discovered, in my innocence, that there was such a thing as fate and that it could take a life and dismember it.

My brother hates it when I use the word fate. But then he is a doctor. He believes that they are bringing fate around, getting it under control. Genetics, for example, now makes it possible to estimate, with varying degrees of accuracy, the time and manner of our dying. In Greek mythology, the Fates determined the length of human life, taking their scissors to our span. We may have the knowledge once reserved by these goddesses, but we haven't much idea how to live with what we know. Would ignorance be better? my brother wants to know.

Wouldn't ignorance leave us happier? I vainly reply.

Since when does happiness have anything to do with it? he says.

*

Whenever I think about fate, that word he despises, I remember a particular set of television images from my childhood. Time-lapse photography was in its infancy then, before the video age of instant replays and slo-mos. I particularly remember a time-lapse film shot in a ballistics lab, where scientists and mathematicians and gun designers were studying the impact of bullets on steel or brick or bone. The spray patterns made by the debris when the bullets exited through the bone were beautiful.

When I try to imagine fate, I think of it as a bullet leaving a smoking chamber, perforating the flesh of our ancestors, exiting in spray and resuming its flight towards the expectant canopy of our skin. Thanks to genetics, we can see the bullet coming, estimate its likely impact and the path it will cut through our viscera. We can even calculate the pattern of the exit spray. The one thing we cannot do is duck.

When I tell my brother this, he says I am talking bad science. We do not know enough. Look at you and me, he says. Ninety-nine per cent the same genetic material. Yet a stranger couldn't tell we were brothers. True enough. I am tall, thin and of gloomy disposition. He is smaller, russet-haired, big chested and of briskly energetic manner. He has strangely small delicate hands. Mine are long, heavily veined and thin. He says as little as he can. Words pour out of me in an anxious, self-justifying stream. I got married, had children. He has stayed single all his life. His calm self-containment is a wonder to me. I feel needy, unreliable and dependent by comparison. We have never exactly understood each other, but a deep unspoken complicity flows between us. I regard this as a mystery. I doubt he has given it a minute's thought.

As a doctor, my brother is untroubled by what he doesn't know. He lives with the fact that there is still no way of predicting what happens after the initial impact of the cue ball, how the reds bank off and carom, how some sink, ow some lose velocity and come to rest on the baize. We do not know how genetics and environment carom off each other. Why should it worry you? he wants to know.

It doesn't worry me, but it does seem ironic that we have just enough knowledge to know our fate, but not enough to do anything to avert it. Genetics now routinely predicts outcomes which medicine can do nothing to prevent. We can identify the children in a particular family who will inherit certain forms of as yet incurable disease. Geneticists call this form of knowledge the new clairvoyance.

My mother did not have the new clairvoyance, just the old foreboding. I was twelve when I asked her what had happened to Nettie. She was making dinner and had her back to me, and she didn't turn round. I can see her, in jeans and a sweatshirt, in front of the stove, the fork in her hand pausing in mid-air.

'Why do you want to know?'

'Just do.'

'It was called hardening of the arteries in the brain.'

'So what can we do?' I ask.

Then her bare feet pivot on the black-and-white tiles of the kitchen, and she says softly:

'You can always stand on your head.'

And so I did. I still do. Every morning I get up and lay a square of towel in front of the wall, kneel down, form a triangle with my elbows and palms, and then kick my legs in the air and find the plumb line of my balance and remain there with the blood flooding into my eyes. When they were small, my son and daughter used to come and watch, tipping themselves upside down so that they could see me right side up, eyes popping out of my head.

'Blood flow has nothing to do with it,' my brother says.

But that's beside the point. I need to do something, anything.

Writing may be like standing on your head; an exercise in magic, a vain exorcism of spirits. At least my wife thinks so. 'Why do you think that writing about it will make any difference?' she says in that quietly lethal way of hers. Her authority over me depends on remarks like that. All I can say is that I won't know until I try.

I could call this the history of my family as the history of our characteristic illness. I could also call it the history of an illness as the history of one family. However, I'm too close to what happened to be a historian. What I have written is more like a time capsule.

Does anyone still remember time capsules?

I still recall every object we placed in the zinc box in the concrete slab at the base of the school flag at Alton High, my senior year in high school:

A 45 of Elvis Presley singing 'Jailhouse Rock', plus a picture of the King.
One pair of nylon stockings.
The Bible.
The Collected Works of Shakespeare.
The Alton senior class yearbook, with a picture of me in it, wearing a pair of winged glasses. My wife came two pages later, with her hair in a bob. We are all smiling, every single one of us.
An RCA transistor radio, with a pink panelled dial.
A copy of *Time* magazine and a pack of Wrigley's spearmint gum.
A complete set of coins – penny, nickel, dime, quarter, dollar – all in mint condition.

Looking back over the list, I can't say we had much imagination. What we did have was faith. Perhaps this was because we were so afraid. Remember, we were the generation of duck and cover drills, hiding under our school desks to shield us from the falling debris of our suburban world. That state of subliminal fear was so pervasive I don't think we even noticed it. It could only surface in projects like the time capsule.

We wanted the future to understand us, since we did not begin to understand ourselves. We believed that our artefacts – especially 'Jailhouse Rock' – would explain us better than we could ourselves. We wanted the future to forgive us for what we might do with our lives. We wanted the future to remember us, and thus to redeem us in our own sight. I can see us all as our teacher trowelled the last of the cement over the box, the shadow that passed across our faces.

So this is my time capsule. What is there? A news-clipping. Photographs. A PET scan. A speech I gave to the Alton Rotarians. A memoir of an illness, as yet not understood. Fragments of a philosophical exercise I wrote in the midst of what was happening and then abandoned when I came to my senses. Then there are some pieces of fiction, some pieces of dialogue, to simulate what happened. My brother would want it known that he never said some of the things I have reported him as saying. But that misses the point. I can't remember exactly what we said, those angry and often desperate evenings, but I can remember the tone of feeling, and I still believe, though he disagrees, that I have been true to what happened. In any event, what strikes me most is how poorly we grasped what was actually happening, how incompletely we must grasp it even now. That is why I call this a time capsule. If someone digs it up in the future, they are bound to say: Look at what they didn't know. Look at what they failed to understand. Look at these curious creatures. Why were they so afraid?

SHE IS WEARING her painting clothes: one of Father's white shirts with the tails tied round her waist, a pair of paint-spattered jeans, and her hair is pulled back off her face in a red band. Her feet are bare and her toenails are painted vermilion. When she comes over and moves a strand of hair off my face, I smell the turpentine on her hands. There is paint under her fingernails. My mother is painting my portrait.

She is working outside in front of the house on the grass under the maple, because it is cool and because she doesn't want me in the studio. The studio is off limits. My father can't abide the fact that he is not allowed in there. The studio is in the barn behind the house and its window, by design, faces the meadow and the hill behind.

One day, when she was working, she caught him peeking in through the studio window. I was up the hill, lying on the grass, and I saw it happen. He was bending over, spying on her, when I saw him recoil, as if he had been slapped, and then slink away back into the house. When I came by the window, the blue splash from her paint tin was still oozing down the pane. Behind the film of paint, I could see her pacing up and down between the rows of finished canvases against the walls, furiously smoking a cigarette.

She is standing in front of her easel, with the palette in her hand, leaning on her back foot, while she considers what to do with me. I am sitting on top of the picnic table under the tree with my bare legs dangling over the edge. I am wearing shorts and a striped T-shirt. I have been posing for two hours a day for a week. Every so often she lets me rest and walk about so I do not get bored. What I'm not allowed to do is look at what she is doing. She says it upsets her concentration.

Her concentration is like a mosquito net, which she draws down over the two of us, excluding everyone else. My brother is lying in the hammock on the porch, reading a first-year med. school textbook and pretending to ignore us. He affects not to care that it is my portrait that she is painting, not his.

My father circles around the lawn in his bathing suit, watching us and trimming the hedge with a pair of pruning shears. When he circles in to have a look, she nudges him out of the way with her hip. If I had this moment on video, I would play it over and over: the way her hip moves and how he fakes grabbing at her, then stands back, looking happy. 'Get us a beer,' she says, and he goes up the veranda steps. I hear the screen door slam, and I hear him singing inside the house, and then he emerges, slapping a mosquito off his shoulder.

She hums quietly, and paces to and fro, oblivious to everyone else, trying to get the measure of my face.

Children are impossible, she says, and when I ask her why she says it is because their faces are always changing. Like light among clouds. Dammit, she swears softly and lights a cigarette. My father puts a beer into her free hand and she takes a long sip while he tosses one to my brother in the hammock.

'Give the boy one too.'

'So young ?' my father says.

I am fourteen. I want to have Miles Davis's fine bones. I want to play the slide guitar like Elmore James. I want my face to stop changing, my voice to settle down into something strong and masculine. I want to be a man of few words. I want to drink. My father looks me over, then tosses me my first can and when I open it, it gushes over my hands.

I am as old now as she was then. I can still smell the hops and feel the chill of the can between my fingers. I am still addicted to impossible wishes. I am still trying to remember every single instant of the days my mother painted my portrait.

'Stop posing,' she says.

'I'm not.'

'I don't care what you want to look like.'

'I just want to look good.'

'Who says you won't?'

'Just don't make me look sensitive.'

She lights another cigarette, exhales, squints over the top of her brush, which she holds out in front of her, and then makes a short, decisive stroke. I feel the beam of her concentration upon my eyes and I can see the brush in her left hand drawing my sockets with quick, semicircular motions. She stops, dabs at the stroke with a rag, stands back, takes a quick drag on the cigarette and closes in again for a rectifying gesture. A portrait is all about eyes. 'Get those right, and you're home,' she says, then 'Damn,' and dabs at the stroke with a rag. Again, she pauses, appraises me, darts to the canvas and stands back. She leans her weight on her back leg and studies the result. She laughs. 'I gave you the damn things,' she says, meaning my eyes, which are shaped like hers. 'I should be able to get them right.' But my eyes elude her for most of the week. When something eludes her, she sings some Judy Garland: soft, and always flat.

For years I've had it preached to me
And drummed into my head
Unless you've played the Palace
You might as well be dead.

She begins working on the background with a palette knife and from where I sit, I can see the back of the canvas bowing as it takes the pressure of the blade. She holds the colour on the knife and then applies it in sharp downward slashes. I also see her glancing up over the top of the canvas, checking out some detail of my face. I look away.

'What are you frightened of?'

'Nothing.'

Now I understand. We had struck a bargain, though I didn't know it at the time. I would have her all to myself for a week. In return, I had to surrender to her scrutiny. I had to give myself to her without reserve. That was the deal. And of what she had seen, she would reveal only what she chose to depict. While she was working, I wasn't allowed to look. At the end of each session, she packed away the canvas and the easel in the studio and locked the door.

'Your face is difficult,' she says. Only her eyes are visible, appraising me, above the top of the canvas.

'No, it's not.'

'You keep hiding.'

'I'm here.'

'No, you're not.'

Second by second, she monitors my concentration, willing me to return to that state of attention, of being there and nowhere else, that she requires. Once or twice, she comes over and puts the flat of one palm on my chest and the flat of the other on my back and moves me bodily a quarter inch to the right, like a vase. 'Now don't move.'

Back at the canvas, she grins. 'There. There. Hold it,' she says.

'You sound like the school photographer.'

'Photography is what this is not, kid. Stop talking. Stop turning back. There. Stay right there. Good. Good.' She moves quickly, darting in to the canvas, jabbing with the brush, then the palette knife, then a corner of rag to slur something, to add a certain texture. She is bisected by the canvas. Above it, I see her appraising blue eyes, below it, when the work is going well, I see her bare feet keeping the beat to the song she is humming to herself.

At the time I took the fact that she managed to paint me as a sign that I was her favourite. Now I know that this was not the case. She probably loved my brother best. She did try to paint him, but it never worked. He resisted her. He was nineteen, just off to med. school, straining to break free – or that is how I see it now – and not inclined to submit to a week of her scrutiny. Since he refused to sit for her, she did some sketches when he was lolling in the hammock, or when we were throwing a frisbee on the lawn, or when we swam naked in the pond. I can see her now, on the deck chair on the veranda, with a pencil between her teeth, chalking on her sketch pad. It was how she committed everything important to memory: with deft, strong marks in charcoal which made a searing sound across white paper.

My mother painted me, not because I was closest to her, but because I was emotionally manageable. She was too close to my brother, and, in another way, too close to my father to turn them into subjects for her work. She knew what she thought about me and so she could paint me without being uncertain of her vantage point.

'How did you know what she thought of you?' my brother says. 'How do you know a thing like that?' I just knew.

One afternoon, under the maple, in a dusky, humid moment, with thunder clouds gathering behind the house, she tossed her paintbrush down onto the palette, picked up a rag, wiped her hands and walked up to the house. Over her shoulder she said, 'It's finished.'

I had expected something different. In the photographs from that time, I always have the same foolish rubbery grin of the kid brother, the youngest son, with someone's large hand round my waist. In the picture I like best, I am sitting on my father's shoulders, my heels against his large, tightly stretched belly, my hands gripping the wiry grey hair at the back of his head, my face grinning with mad anxiety. I cannot remember any of the scenes these photographs record, but sometimes now, in late middle age, I wake up in the morning knowing that in the night I have been back to some scene in front of that house. It is summer. The garden sprinkler is on. My mother is singing and I can hear her through the open window of the studio. My father is making coffee in the kitchen and is listening to the overnight baseball scores on the radio. The day will be long and hot.

In my portrait, as I discovered when I came round the easel for my first look, she made me sad and downcast, staring inwards, oblivious to the bright blue sky she has painted round my head. My father came down the porch steps and we stood for a while looking at it. Even now, I can feel his hand on my right shoulder. He looks for a long time. 'So,' is all he says, as if he is as surprised as I am. It is the portrait of a child watching his childhood vanish before his eyes.

I came into the kitchen, where she was making herself

a cup of tea, and asked her why she had painted me looking so gloomy. She said, 'Your face in repose looks sad.' And I can remember thinking: Am I sad? I don't feel sad. How did she know? In her picture, I get to see myself through her eyes, and I think that it takes me about as deep into myself as I am ever likely to go. Looking at it now – it hangs in my bedroom – I find it strange that forty years on I have changed so little. All the cells in my body have been replaced a number of times, and I have had a life. Nevertheless I remain what I was when she painted me.

She once said to me – we were talking about my father – 'You know, there are some people who just find living *hard.*' At the time I didn't know what she was talking about. How can life be hard? Gravity is the same for all of us, even him. Now I think she also meant people like me, people whose faces in repose are sad.

She never seemed to find life hard. She lived her life with the ease of a born swimmer, unlike my father who seemed to live as if he was fording an icy stream. This had much to do with his life in exile, whereas she spent most of her life within fifteen miles of Alton. He was often tormented by regret, but I never heard her say she regretted anything. Her self-sufficiency was just something each of us, especially my father, had to accept. She painted because she loved to paint. She never exhibited. She had no career, no ambitions for her work except that it be good, and she didn't care what we thought of it.

I can see her diving into the pond behind the house, then pulling herself out and sneaking up behind Father's lawn chair and deftly squeezing the water out of her long, blonde braid down my father's back. Father roars and chases her around the grass; she dodging, ducking, he lunging, closing in at the pond's edge, so that she takes his hand, as if they are about to start jiving, then pivots and chucks him in. When he comes out roaring, covered in mud and weeds, he shouts, 'You bloody woman,' and she imitates his accent perfectly, 'Blady vooman,' clapping her hands, dodging expertly as he gives chase again, beating him back to the porch door and slamming it in his face.

My wife thinks I am enslaved to these memories, and that they made me more retrospective and melancholy than I should have been. 'You're not all here,' she often said to me. Nemesis of a happy childhood, I should have replied.

We moved up to the farm from the city, I now see, when the chemical company gave my father a promotion and when the money from Nettie's will came through. My mother had grown up in Alton and didn't want to come back to live there, but when the Fraser place came up and she saw that my father had got it into his head to buy it, she knew it was hopeless to resist. 'The barn will be your studio,' he promised her. 'The attic will be my study. You will see.'

Every Friday night for three years, from April to September, he changed out of his suit, put on his overalls and drove up the highway to work on the place. I was in grade school then, and sometimes I went up with him and held ladders for him and got the nails ready and served up the coffee, while he worked away, swearing, whistling to himself, battling to bring the old Fraser place back from the dead. I see him stripped to the waist on a ladder banging in shingles, singing in off-key Russian, the songs garbled by the nails in his mouth.

'I know this house better than I know myself,' my father would say. It is probably true that the things you make with your own hands are the parts of yourself you come closest to understanding. My books, for example. I know why they're no better than they are, whereas I can't begin to explain why I myself am no better than I am.

It was that dark-stained clapboard farmhouse in two and a half acres of pasture that allowed my father his deepest form of self-expression. Having re-wired it, rolled insulation through every cavity, sanded the boards and fitted new windows, he was entitled to treat the place as if it was an extension of his own nervous system. When he wasn't upstairs in his study, typing out reports, analyses and reviews for the *Journal of Soils Chemistry*, he was wandering about with a screwdriver or a paintbrush in his back pocket, fixing and repairing something. His ears detected a loose screw in the porch door or a drip in the basement tap before any of the rest of us. This relentless tinkering was the way a man like him, not much given to self-reflection, made his stand against the mortality of things.

There were times as a teenager when I couldn't understand what a shy, thoughtful woman like my mother saw in a man like him. Now I realise that she deferred to his sheer animal energy. And to the fact that he was different. When they met, he was, in his own words, a 'dumb bohunk, with no English,' driving a gravel truck in Alton to get the money to finish graduate school. He laid the gravel in the school driveway, and that was how they met, because she came out of the lunchroom to look. When he finished tipping the gravel, she said, as a joke, 'No one wears shorts like that,' looking at his absurd, semi-obscene short shorts, which gave him away as a European. After all, this was Alton, circa 1936 and there was nothing like him in fifty miles. He strutted a pace or two for her and offered her a cigarette, and she said she couldn't because she had to go back inside and teach, and he came back at the end of the day and took her out for a drive, barrelling up the dirt concession roads in a clapped-out Ford that didn't have a single window, or so she remembered, which rolled up properly. I think she was surprised, and proud in a way, that she had married someone so unlike herself.

None of the pieces of his nature fitted together: the gravel truck and the good manners, the short shorts and the degree in soils chemistry, the habit of never wearing a shirt outdoors in warm weather and the quiet precision of his work in the company lab. Beneath all the surface noise – 'I am surrounded by idiots, especially you, you ridiculous boy' etc etc – he was a meticulous and careful man. She deferred to that. As for his rages, she accepted them as the thundery weather necessary to a certain kind of exotic jungle vegetation. I saw him make her cry, from sheer spite, once or twice, and I couldn't forgive him for that. But she did forgive him. Forgiveness was her prerogative, and she knew how to make him beg for it.

She had trouble getting her words out and he was merciless about that, as if it was a flaw that both provoked and frightened him. Often, as a teenager, I did not understand what she was saying. Sentences would begin and stutter to a halt. Words spilled out of her in a jumble.

'What it was when they came for the picture thing was that there was no one at home and so I said I wouldn't wait just got into the truck and went off without thinking.' I wrote that one down so that I would remember it afterwards.

To follow what she said, you had to scurry after her, filling in the blanks, rearranging the clauses. It was as if her thoughts came too fast to be fixed down in words.

'Oh you know what I mean,' she would exclaim whenever I looked puzzled, as if it would put an end to the fun of talking altogether if she had to go back and explain herself. Her difficulties made her respect articulate people more than she should have done. When my brother graduated from medical school in Boston, she was so impressed I had to remind her he wasn't Einstein.

'Yes, but I only went to teachers' training college,' she replied.

Her rambling speech would exasperate my father beyond measure. 'What are you trying to express?' he would say. 'What thought is struggling from your brain?'

She knew she had a problem. 'Why do you think I paint?' she said once, by way of explanation. It was her primary language, the one that never failed her. So much so that if she had to give you directions, she would start in words, and then say, 'Forget it, give me a pencil,' and draw you a map, complete with the drive-in on the left, and the Safeway on the hill, and two tamarisk trees in the garden of the house on the corner where you were to take the left.

She could write her first name and her married name simultaneously with her left and right hands. She could do this any way you chose: first name descending vertically below the line, second name ascending vertically or the other way. If she pursed her lips and concentrated harder, she could write them backwards simultaneously with both hands. These party tricks left us with the impression that the wiring of her circuits was different from ours. I am sure that she cultivated these minor talents to reserve some margin of inscrutability from the three of us.

The larger mystery is why she suddenly stopped painting. My brother was away at medical school. Father was away in the city. I was finishing Alton High. The two of us were alone in the house. I saw it happen.

The last canvas she completed was a copy of Andrea Mantegna's *Christ Descending into Limbo*, a painting she had only ever seen in a reproduction in a book which my father brought back for her from a business trip to New York. She had never copied a painting before, but I remember she spent weeks working on it in her studio. I would find her there when the school bus dropped me off at the end of the day, still standing where I had left her in the morning, with the Mantegna reproduction on the stand by the easel.

In the original, Christ is about to descend into a dark grotto to rescue the lost souls in purgatory. She stripped the composition of all religious signification and darkened the tonality of the painting, using the same reds and blacks and ochres as Mantegna but making the elements in the original her own. A mysterious, half-finished figure seen from behind is looking back towards a cave, cut into a dark mountain. At the entrance to the cave stand two women beckoning to the figure in the foreground. Mother used a smoke-washed shade of purple of the summer sky at dusk for the figures. For the cave, at the centre of the painting, she chose black.

The painting hangs in my brother's study in Boston. If you get up close, you can see the exact place where her last brush stroke juddered to a stop, each fibre in the brush imprinted onto the paint by the pressure of her hand. This was the stroke which completed the head of the figure whose back is turned to the viewer. I've always believed this half-hidden figure was the only self-portrait she ever attempted. When she had completed it, she never painted again.

I BLAMED MY FATHER for having made my mother give up her painting. I thought he had been more infantile and possessive than a powerful and successful adult should have been. So I said this to him. Or rather I said, She used to paint. Not any more. She has wishes for you and for me and my brother, but none for herself. Not any more.

I don't believe he ever forgave me for that. I can still see my father's hands covering his face, as if he was sheltering from a blow.

'I think you should go now. Get out. Get out.'

I did. I boarded in a rooming house in the city. I completed my first year in college. It was a year before I came back.

I wonder whether either of us had any grip on the truth at all. Then I thought my father took up all the oxygen in the room. Now I realise that his great strength was the naïve candour and power of all his longings.

My memory resists me. I can't seem to bring him back as he was. He remains in pieces in my mind, a rough-hewn, innocent man well over six feet tall with steel wire hair that stood up on the back of his head and seemed to add an inch to his height. What else? An axe scar on his left knee, elegant hands that ran through the wiry hair on the back of his head whenever he was puzzled or annoyed, oddly small and delicate feet for someone so large. I can't begin to enumerate all his contradictions. He was a believer all his life yet had no faith in an afterlife. 'He watches over you, while you're alive, but when you go, that's it,' he once said to me. He cursed her vigorously – 'that fucking woman' – yet punished us if we swore. He had a furious temper and hated himself for it. I can still see him on his knees, with his head in my mother's lap, entirely unembarrassed, whispering sorry sorry sorry. She smokes a cigarette and angrily ignores him.

He laughed heartily when anyone told a vulgar story, yet was incapable of telling one himself; he affected to be a man of action and had no time for 'ideas'. 'You are too vague, boy. It is useless what you are thinking. Useless.' But he was an incorrigible theoriser himself. All theories fascinated him, from continental drift to those of my brother's neurology, and he would sit up late at night, if one of his sons was willing to provide a silent audience, and argue the merits of these theories in tireless monologues.

Women found him attractive, but he never carried on with them. He was a classically uxorious man, vain, demanding, imperious with her, yet a prisoner of her moods and whims. He could appear boundlessly self-confident and arrogant at one moment and utterly defenceless the next. My mother once found him upstairs lying on the bed with his hands over his face whispering, 'Worthless, completely worthless'. She told me this story without embarrassment, as if she admired the candour of his desperation.

In his shorts, with the screwdrivers in the back pocket, he looked like a repairman. In his dinner jacket, dressed for the company banquet, he could pass for a patrician. Although he had changed his name, you could still hear Odessa in his voice.

'You are going, boy?'

'Yes, I am going.'

'Why are you not embracing me?'

'I embrace you.'

'As a son should.'

As a son should. He disapproved of my yearnings, my vagueness, my longing to have some kind of expressive or examined life, like mother's. 'You should have a profession. And a pension.' Only an émigré and an exile could have been so doggedly unimaginative about his son's life. Now I see that he just wanted to spare me his own hard beginnings.

I tried lots of alternatives to the steady life he wanted for me, but the drip, drip of his scorn for my experiments eventually wore me down. I ended up, as he wished, with a profession and a pension. And a doctorate too. I was a dutiful son, and a competitive one. He had a doctorate himself, in soils chemistry, and there was my brother, a medical researcher. Three men all competing, mostly for her favour.

As my father used to say, 'Your brother has a propositional intelligence.' Meaning, he got perfect scores in every math test he ever took. Meaning he had a way of reasoning that viewed ordinary life and its problems from an altitude of 40,000 feet. Whereas, my father said, I had 'an autobiographical intelligence', which was his way of saying I had a scatty female mind, interested in gossip and personal details and stories and character, things he didn't have time for. Father had so little of the autobiographical sort that he wouldn't have remembered making the distinction in the first place.

He would say, 'You take after your mother, boy,' but I knew this. I didn't need him to attribute it to me like some destiny which chalked out the circle of the rest of my life. I had the right, the same as he did, to find out what I was good for, without him laying down the answer in advance.

I don't know why I clung to all my grievances. Perhaps they were all I had at that age. Fighting with him gave me proof that I was something more than a son. Yet a son I have remained.

Now that it is too late, I see him and me clearly, illuminated in the slanting rays of time. There were thirty-four years between us, a world war and a revolution. His memory began at a window overlooking the Black Sea on a February morning in 1917. 'I am too small to look out of the window. So I get a chair and I can hear the noise it makes as I pull it across the parquet. Same word in Russian: Parquet. I open window. I am looking down, and on the boulevard sailors, everywhere. One throws his cap into the air and it nearly reaches me.' That sailor's cap is there, between us, hovering in the air, almost the only thing he ever told me about his childhood.

His first memory is from Eisenstein, mine from some film noir starring Barbara Stanwyck and Richard Widmark. We have pulled into a filling station on the road between Alton and the city. I see the old style gas pumps and the Flying Horse sign creaking in the wind. I am coming on for three; my brother is not there and I have my parents all to myself. The wipers are scraping across the bubbling sheet of water on the windscreen. The rain is drumming on the body of the car, the world is on the other side of the water and I am looking up into my mother's face. She is laughing. I am safe.

My father's childhood was never safe. He saw prisoners being dragged in halters behind horses through the streets of Odessa during the civil war. He remembered sitting on the family's luggage at the dock side in Constantinople in May 1919 when his father reached into his back pocket and discovered that his wallet – with all their money – was gone. His moods were always given legitimacy by his original dispossession. Exile became a set of emotional permissions we were all bound to respect. He got away with murder.

'Why did you marry him?' I once asked my mother

'What am I supposed to say?' she replied. 'Because he would not take no for an answer.' There were times when I felt she had betrayed me by marrying him.

I can't re-enter my earlier self. Even my anger, once so fierce, now seems false and invented to me. It has become a phantom, another of my losses. As I look back, I think we were actually fighting – though neither of us realised it at the time – about who was to blame for what was happening to her. As if either of us was actually to blame.

Once she stopped painting, something happened. I can't find the words for it for at first the change was barely perceptible. I can't even remember what I thought at the time. Now, I think she lost the secret source of her calm and self-containment. Some inner certainty slowly ebbed away.

At the dinner table, her features would glaze over for a second, and she would cease to attend to the conversation. When she saw you watching, she would snap back into the world with a tiny shiver of her shoulders and leap up and begin clearing the plates from the table.

'What are you staring at?'

'Nothing, Mother.'

She would get up from the table, and her hand would go to the small of her back, to ease some new twinge there. She would brush the hair off her face and I would see a few streaks of silver.

'You look terrific,' I would say.

'You liar,' she would reply.

She had always loved making time stretch and expand, so that lunch might start about one and still be staggering to a more or less drunken conclusion around four in the afternoon. Now she wanted to get meals over with, so that she would even reach over to take your plate away before you had finished eating. If you said, 'What's the hurry?' she would stop, between kitchen and the table, with a plate in her hand, and you could see her thinking 'Why am I like this?'

Suddenly she seemed pinched and drawn, even slightly stooped.

I said, 'How are you, Mum?'

'Fine.'

'Just asking.'

'So I'm telling you.'

Once she said, 'Old age ain't for cowards, kid,' before disappearing into the kitchen to wash a pot or peel a potato.

'You aren't old.'

'Huh,' she said, dismissively, pointing her toe in a ballet stance, then rocking back on her heel in a half-hearted little step, as if there was a protesting part of her that still wanted to dance.

Ageing was what it was, of course, but ageing has an infinity of gradients. My father was eight years older than she was, just coming up to retirement, but it was as if he remained on a plateau, whereas she was slipping down a steep ramp. She made his meals, clipped her roses, weeded the flowerbeds, but now lived within a silence broken only by firm remarks that pushed our concerns away. There was never a word of complaint. She was the kind of lapsed Presbyterian who had to be in a speechless fever before she would allow us to put her to bed.

I blamed my father for what was happening. When he retired from the company, his demands on her became impossible. I told him their marriage had become a prison to her. He told me their marriage was none of my business. He said I was behaving like an adolescent, which I certainly was. But now I wonder whether he understood any better than I did. As a man whom exile had taught that there was nothing you couldn't overcome if you set your mind to it, the feeling that she was slipping away from him was more than he could bear.

I remember the night my mother's elder sister suddenly died. Father took the call and then went out to my mother who was bent over one of the flowerbeds. I saw him kneel down beside her, whisper and then try to stroke her hair. She put the clippers down on the stone and then, as she got to her feet, she pushed his hand away. She walked past him into the orchard. For an hour, he stood on the porch, watching her walk up and down, a small bent figure in the distance.

That night they both went to bed early, and I stayed up to watch a lightning storm, moving across the valley like a procession of Chinese dragons. I sat watching from my upstairs window, leaning against the wall. A lamp above my head twirled in the draught. The house was holding the heat of the day like perfume in a discarded shawl.

Illuminated by flashes of lightning, I saw my mother standing by the back-porch door, looking out at the fields. I wanted to go out to her, I even thought she might be in some danger, because the lightning was close. But the look on her face kept me where I was. A gust of rain spattered the dust at her feet, and she moved her hand to her face and felt the drops on her forehead. Then with the lightning flashing all round her, she began walking out into the field; now there, now gone, now there, now gone, now livid silver, now black shadow. I felt an aching certainty that she was going to walk across the fields to the road at the bottom and that she would follow the road out to the highway until she had walked right out of her life.

But that is not what happened. After half an hour, she

turned back to the house. She came towards me, up the dark path past the pond, her head down, her eyes in shadow. Only my light was showing, and I was going to wave and say something, when I realised she hadn't seen me at all. She walked past my window, across the gravel and shut the door of the house behind her.

MOTHER IS LEANING back in her chair on the porch with a wineglass in her hand watching the light dwindling away behind the poplars. After a time she says, 'I never expected anything like this. The stone wall that Dad built for us, the hedges, the studio, the house. It's all turned out so well.'

I am sitting beside her, but she might as well be talking to herself. Her voice is mournful and far away. I can't think of anything to say. It is painful to remember this silence now. She needed comfort and I had none to give her.

The lights come on in Alton, just visible through the trees. She twirls her wineglass between her fingers and she says, out of nowhere, 'When I was ten, my father said, "Who remembers the opening of the Aeneid?" as he stood at the end of the table carving the Sunday joint. "Anyone?" They were all better scholars than me, but I knew. "Arma virumque cano . . . " Of arms and the man I sing. Nettie put down her knife and fork and just stared at me. I wasn't supposed to be the clever one.'

She gets up, drains her glass and then smiles bitterly. 'Nettie always said, "Never make a fuss." That was the family rule.' So we will not make a fuss.

Then she whispers, 'Have you seen my glasses?'

'Your glasses don't matter. You can see without them.'

'I know they don't matter. But if he finds out . . . '

'Tell him to . . . ' Now I'm the one who is whispering. He mustn't find out. We must carry on as if nothing is amiss. She disappears inside. Through the picture window I can see her rummaging behind the sofa cushions. She picks up a book by the reading lamp, opens the silver cigarette case on the mantelpiece. She doesn't have a clue where to look and I can't bear to watch.

When I find her glasses by the night table in her bedroom, the lenses are fogged and smudged with fingerprints.

She wipes them on her sleeve and says, 'I know. It runs in the family.'

'What does?'

She gives me a hard stare. 'Dirty glasses. Nettie always said Dad washed his in his soup.'

Why doesn't she buy herself a second pair of glasses? Why is she losing her capacity to defend herself?

I take her into Alton and in the Drugmart I buy her a chain so she can wear them round her neck. She submits with good grace while Al Jackman the pharmacist slips the chain over her head, but in the car on the way back she is furiously silent, and when we come up the driveway, she suddenly shakes her fist at the windscreen and whispers, 'I swore I'd never wear one of these goddamned things.'

'Why?' I say, as we pull up in front of the house.

'Nettie wore her glasses on a chain,' she says hoarsely, pushing her shoulder angrily against the car door to get out.

First, the glasses, then the purse. Then the shoes. After that, the pots left boiling on the stove. After that, a roast left to carbonise itself in the oven. I began spending most weekends up at the farm, cooking for both of them, recovering the now interminable list of lost objects, trying to keep him from torturing her about her forgetfulness.

'Your glasses are where you left them this morning,' he says cruelly.

'So where is that?' she hisses at him, at bay.

'Here they are, dear,' I say, putting the chain over her head.

'Don't "dear" me.'

Both of them are too proud to admit what is happening. Yet she must know. When did the moment of insight occur? When exactly did she begin to understand?

I imagine her standing in the studio, with the Mantegna reproduction open on the table, her brush poised in front of the central figure looking back into the beckoning darkness. Prussian blue is the colour on the tip of the brush. There is a stroke to make. Her hand moves forward and then she stops. The instant that connects wishing and doing, linking movement of a hand from palette to brush to canvas, begins to vibrate like a thread under tension. The thread glistens, hums as it is pulled. Suddenly it snaps. She realises instantly that she does not know how to go on. For her there is no such thing as innocent forgetting.

I come up from the city on Friday nights after work and we cook dinner together in the kitchen. She says, 'Where's that thing . . . you . . . flip . . . things . . . with?'

'Spatula,' I say and she gives me a look.

So when she says, 'Where's that thing, you know, that you . . . ' I just put it in her hand.

And then a third time.

'Spatula,' I say.

'So kind,' she says, with a hard sideways glare. Half way through dicing a carrot her hands stop. I come over behind her and take the knife out of her hands. 'Hey,' she says, and grabs the knife back. And then it happens again, an action mysteriously draining away into nothingness.

Father's initial response is to envelope her in a deadening solicitude. 'Here is your purse, darling. Let me hang on to it.'

She looks at him, holding her purse and says archly, 'You look perfectly ridiculous. Give it to me.'

'If I give it to you, you will lose it, my darling.'

'What is this "darling" stuff? Stop being ridiculous. Give it to me.'

Five minutes later, she loses it again.

'What do you need it for?' he pleads. 'You're at home. Where do you think you're going?'

She puts her hand to her face. 'Just tell me where my goddamned purse is.'

The needle circles round and round, stuck in the groove. It can go on for hours, until you want to take her in your arms and shake her. Stop it, Mother. Forget your purse. Forget everything.

One evening after she goes upstairs to bed, my father and I are sitting together in the wicker chairs on the front porch, looking through the orchard to the concession road beyond. I say I can't figure out how much she knows and how much she doesn't.

'She knows,' he says, staring into his whiskey, his voice heavy and tired.

'It's amazingly complicated,' I say, wanting to explore what kind of awareness this could be, of time breaking down inside your head, of no longer even being aware that you are forgetting. But my father snaps, 'Son, it is not interesting at all. I don't know why you talk like this. It is horrible.'

We sit silently until it is pitch-dark, starless and cold. Then he says, 'We must get her to a doctor.'

'What do we need a doctor for? We know what it is.'

'No, no.' He is adamant. 'Scientifically, it is not clear.' Whenever he says that word, he is saying he wants to take the matter out of my hands, out of the realm of empty philosophical talk, into the realm of exactitude and precision where only he and my brother are allowed admission.

'So what is in doubt "scientifically"?' I say.

'Don't be smart with me.'

'Just tell me.'

'We have menopause, change of life.'

'Don't be ridiculous.'

In the darkness, he says vehemently, 'We are not sure. Not yet anyway. She is having a very bad phase. We must persuade her to have tests.'

I tell him he is playing for time, and he says he is tired of me telling him what to do. 'And what about Nettie?' I ask.

'There is a family disposition. But nothing is certain.'

'Scientifically.'

He says nothing, then slaps his knee and clears away a mosquito.

'The car accident. You were too young to remember.'

What does he mean, I am too young to remember? More film noir, this time at speed: my father's face in profile wearing a fedora, my mother beside him in a white spring frock, my brother looking out of the window, and me in the back seat. I am saying something, but I can't hear what it is.

Everything that comes next is confused: the chrome grille of a black Desoto suddenly veering out of lane, coming across the white lines towards us on the two-lane blacktop, Father swerving, and the slow, elephantine dance of everything towards the dull weight of impact, glass splintering and the sky pouring into the car, my head like a flower on a stalk snapped against headrest. And then silence. I sit up in the back seat. My father's head is against the steering wheel, my brother's body is through the windscreen, and I can see his legs draped down the dashboard. My mother's head is flat against the chrome radio, as if she is listening with her ear pinned to the sound. I am saying something over and over. I hear words reverberating in my head, but I cannot figure out what they are. Nobody moves. Everything is perfectly still, framed by the jagged glass of the shattered windscreen.

'I have been talking to your brother about this,' my father is saying.

'About what?'

'The accident.'

'So what does he say?'

'He's coming up Saturday.'

My brother was living in Boston by then, completing his neurological residency. Since he rarely comes home, Mother is excited to see him. It is a rare event for all of us – my wife, my son and my brother – to be all at the same table. We help with dinner but conspire to let Mother feel she has done it herself. We toast her and she says,

'Do you remember Antigonish?'

No one knows why she is saying this, but we all nod. 'You' – pointing to me – 'were three, and you' – pointing at my brother – 'were eight, no nine – and we picnicked on the rocks.'

'And you painted the bluffs,' my father says.

'And I hunted for crabs among the rocks,' my brother says.

'I don't remember any of this,' I say.

'You' – she points at me – 'were three, and you' – she points at my brother – 'were eight and, what's wrong?'

'Nothing, Mother.'

'And you painted the bluffs,' my father says.

'And I hunted crabs,' my brother says.

My mother looks at all of us, and there is a pause. My

father takes her hand and says, 'And I decided to dive in,' and my brother cuts in, looking at her,

'And Dad came up out of the water, clutching himself and shouting, "My vital parts! My vital parts!" '

'Your what?' she says.

'Because it was so cold,' my brother says, but she still looks puzzled and gets up and begins clearing away the table before we can stop her. Five minutes later, she comes back in, wiping her hands on her apron. Her face brightens at the sight of my brother. 'Remember Antigonish?' she says.

After dinner, my father takes her up to bed, my wife goes upstairs with Jack on her shoulder, and my brother and I sit out on the porch, looking up into the sky, watching the night flights heading into the city. After a while, he says, 'I had no idea.'

I feel like shouting at him. What does he mean, he had no idea? I've phoned him a hundred times.

Father comes out with three cups of tea, which he hands out as he sinks into his favourite porch chair. For a while, we sip tea in silence, looking up at the stars. Then he says suddenly, 'I know what she goes through. Don't think I don't. You wake up some mornings and you don't know where the hell you are. Just like a child.' My father sounds angry, as if neither of us could possibly understand.

'I can imagine,' I said.

'Can you really?'

There is a long silence. Of course I cannot imagine. Father pulls himself up out of his chair and goes upstairs to lie beside her.

On Antigonish beach, I see him walking ahead of me in those white plastic bathing shoes of his, following the line of the water's edge, head down, bending now and again to pick up a shell or a stone. He stops to show me what he has found, then throws it away again into the surf. Soon he has vanished into the glare, and I call his name, but he cannot hear.

The next day, because my brother is there, my father gets his lawyer in from Alton to bring out the title deeds he has prepared to transfer to the two of us. We both tell him this can wait, but he insists. The lawyer, a pert young widow, arrives that afternoon and we sit down for business under the maple tree. We examine the deeds of sale. Mother runs a finger over the deeds. "Housewife" sounds ridiculous, doesn't it?' she says, pausing over the way she has been identified.

'How about painter?'

She shakes her head. 'No,' she says. 'Just once more,' she asks, 'tell me why we have to do this.'

'Because,' I reply for what must be the tenth time, 'it is cheaper to transfer the property to us now than doing it afterwards.'

Once the lawyer gathers up the papers with our signatures on them and leaves, I sit on the porch and daydream about hotel rooms: the echo of empty cupboards, the glare of the bathroom mirror, the neon blinking through the shutters, crisp towels and sheets. No object in a hotel room has any claim on you. In hotel rooms, you feel you could start again, be a new person.

Hotels set me thinking of my honeymoon with my wife in Venice at the Hotel San Cassiano in the heat of the afternoon and how we sat cross-legged on the bed, behind closed shutters, listening to the water lapping in the canal below and eating cheese and cherries. Next morning I lay in bed and watched her comb her hair at the dressing table by the open window. A curl of smoke rose from the ashtray and her face flickered in the facets of the mirrors. That might have been the instant I loved her best. Through the window came the sound of water and the droning of a fog horn. We had the whole day ahead of us and for that whole day, I felt we could never be harmed or hurt or diminished by the life ahead. I wonder what she felt. She never said.

But now in the farmhouse, every object has become a hook to catch my thoughts as they pass: the barometers whose portents only he seems to comprehend; the inlaid doors of the corner cupboard bought from the crooked antique dealer outside of Alton; the Iroquois mask made of straw; the Russian bear on a string, hanging from a nail on the kitchen door; a French thermometer marked Moscou 1812 at the cold end and Senegal at the hot end. These objects claim my thoughts and force them to circle at bay.

Next morning when I come down to breakfast in the kitchen, my mother is frying eggs and my son is sitting on my father's lap, playing with his fingers. When Father disengages his hands, I notice that the joints are swollen and that his signet ring is no longer on the little finger of his right hand. He follows my gaze.

'I gave it to your brother. You'll get the watch.'

First the transfer of the property into our names. Then the distribution of personal effects. His first grandchild arrives and he begins making ostentatious preparations for his own departure. What is going on? He strokes his grandson's chest with a tender, absent gesture and then passes him over to my mother.

My mother takes my son and dances him slowly round the kitchen, his soft, child's limbs bouncing on her dressing gown as she croons into his ear, 'Come to me, my melancholy baby.' A look of wild pleasure crosses both their faces.

'You dance well,' my brother says, coming into the room.

She whirls slowly to a stop and hands him back to me:

'No, I always used to lead too much.' Then she comes over and whispers in my son's ear, 'Crazy old granny.'

She remembers captions of *New Yorker* cartoons; lyrics of Broadway shows from the thirties; the name of the little girl with Shirley Temple curls at the desk next to hers at school; the names of all her teachers at Alton High. It is what happened five minutes ago that is slipping away – the pot on the stove, the sprinkler soaking the flowers, the words she just spoke.

She suddenly says, 'I'm sure I will make a cheerful old nut. Don't you think so? In any case,' and here she picks up her coffee and pushes open the screen door onto the porch, 'it'll be much worse for you.'

That night, my wife and I go into Alton to the movies. We return home up the concession road, leaving a plume of dust behind us in the brake lights. She parks the car at the bottom of the driveway and we walk the rest of the way between the pines. She doesn't want to go in, and so we walk past the pond, up through the high grass to the hill behind and lie down with the night sky spread out above us. Down at the house, my brother is reading under the light of the porch lamp and there is a light on in my parents' room. 'It looks like a ship at sea,' she says. I go in search of a name, of a great ship that went down in my childhood, of a great disaster that once held me spellbound. My wife remembers the name before I do. The *Andrea Doria*. She went down off Nantucket in my childhood, after a collision with a freighter, and after they had rescued most of the passengers, they sent divers down and took photographs of her lying in shallow water, with the lights of her bridge, by some impossible chance, still on. The ship's lights streamed through the watery darkness like the livid eyes of a beast staring at the hunter who has brought her down.

As a child, I used to dream about those pictures of the ship glowing on the bottom of the sea. I think of those dreams now as a child's way of imagining what it would be like to die, sinking in the folds of the sea, your eyes blazing in the salty dark. However I imagine death, my eyes are always open.

Lying by my side in the darkness, my wife begins singing to me, Verdi, flat as always.

'I am not flat.'

I am laughing, and she ignores me, singing on in a husky, mocking voice, '*Libera me . . . de morte aeterna.*'

One day soon the house below us in the dark will belong to my brother and me, but no matter what the deeds say, it will always remain theirs. My brother gets up and turns off the lights on the porch. Then my parents' bedroom light is extinguished. The moon goes down and bright cold stars appear. A dog barks. In the house, our child floats in his fathomless sleep. 'Cassiopeia, Ursa Major, Orion's Belt . . . ' I say. 'I must learn the names. I want to teach him the names.'

Out of the dark, as if from far away, she says, 'What do you need to name them for?'

EVERY NIGHT NOW, my father wakes to the sound of mother tiptoeing about in their bedroom, talking to herself. She feels her way out of their room and finds the bannister leading downstairs. He follows and finds her on the sitting room sofa in the dark, with her raincoat over her nightdress, one shoe off and one shoe on, clutching her handbag in her hands, eyes staring at the front door.

Sometimes he can't persuade her to come upstairs and she remains convinced that she has to stay waiting for someone – she can't say whom. One morning, I came down to breakfast and found them both asleep on the sofa in their nightclothes, side by side, holding hands, their heads on each other's shoulders.

He had always appeared to depend upon her in a manner that strangers found touching. He would stroke her arm in the street, nuzzle her in the Alton diner and whisper diminutives in her ear. In public her manner with him was regal and amused, in private ever so slightly distant. Her distance provoked him and from time to time he would explode, showering her with curses.

Now she was the one who clung to his arm, who feared at every moment that he was going to leave her for ever. The reversal was so complete, I feared sometimes that he might run away. But he didn't. He just gave up wanting what she used to give him. He stopped being the domineering child of the family and became her father and her nurse.

He put on the apron in the mornings, prepared her meals,

assembled her clothing, retrieved her lost handbag for the thousandth time, placed the glasses on a chain around her neck, smoothed her hair with his hand and in a myriad of ways, maintained the outward façade of her life. All the while, he continued to turn out book reviews and technical studies from the little study in the attic. He was categorical on one point: as long as he lived, he would never abandon her. By which he meant he would never put her in any kind of an institution. At first I thought his devotion was the tribute paid to the love he used to feel for her. Now I realise that illness drew them closer. Faded and blurred though she was, she never abandoned him either. Once in a while, as if waking up from a sleep, she would look at him, take his face in her hands and kiss him on the forehead or cheek. He would bend his head, silently, gratefully submitting to a mystery.

I was now spending every weekend up at the farm, helping out. Our daughter had just been born, and my wife stayed in the city to look after her. Whichever way I turned in those years, I knew I was bound to desert or betray somebody. On Friday nights, when I got home from work, I changed and went up to the farm, leaving my wife to cope with two children alone. On Sunday nights, when I got in the car to drive back to the city and prepare my classes, I felt I was abandoning my father. So it went, the tear in the fabric of my life getting larger year by year. My brother was never there, and when I phoned him in Boston to tell him what was happening to Mother, he always sounded distracted, as if I was interrupting something more important.

The summer my father retired from the company, he was invited to a soils conference in Denver and I told him to go. He needed a rest. I told him I would bring Jack up with me and we would look after her together.

Within five minutes of Father's departure, the questions begin.

'Where is Dad?'

'He is out now, but he'll be back soon.'

'That's wonderful,' she says. Three minutes later she looks puzzled,

'But Dad . . . '

'He's away at work, but he'll be back later.' I haven't got it in me to tell her that he is going to be away for two weeks. 'And what are you doing here? I mean it's nice, but . . . '

'I'm your son, for Chrissake.' I'm laughing when I say this.

'I see.'

At first, I try to count the number of times she asks these questions. On the first day, I lose track at sixty-three.

She remembers what it felt like when the Model T Ford ran into her at the school gates when she was a girl of seven. She remembers the summer nights when her father used to wrap her in a blanket and take her out to the edge of Otter Lake to see the stars. But she can't dice an onion. She can't boil a kettle of water. Any sustained course of action requires more concentration than she can muster. Cold curiosity leads me to ask her to set the table, just to see what will happen. She puts the knife where the fork ought to be, a plate with neither knife nor fork, and a spoon far off in the middle of the table. She looks bored with the result.

Jack is just learning to write his name on his eraser board. He erases the first letters of his name with his left hand, while writing the last letters of his name with his right hand. It seems to fascinate him, as if he is experimenting with his own disappearance. It is also as if he is miming what it is like to be with his grandmother. No matter what he says, a hand keeps erasing his words from the board of her mind.

In the old days, she played cards with a cigarette between her lips and a lightning eye to the main chance. Now my son lays out his animal cards for a game of pairs on the dining room table and quickly finds a pair of penguins. She just turns up cards at random.

My son gets impatient. 'You're not playing properly,' he shouts, punches her arm and runs from the table. My mother looks after him, with a wounded expression, conscious of his disappointment, but unaware of its cause. She says gently, 'Don't run around quite so much.'

I pull him back to the table and tell him to apologise. He decides to kiss her feet. She smiles down at him and says, 'Oh your kisses are so full of sugar.'

Ten minutes later, she comes into the kitchen with a puzzled look on her face. She points to Jack playing on the floor with a tractor and whispers,

'He's a nice little boy. Where does he sleep, I mean, who does he belong to?'

All the time now, she looks frightened. I hold her hand, tell her I am here, and that she has nothing to worry about. But it makes no difference. Sometimes she looks at me and I know she is struggling to remember who I am.

I invite four old friends from Alton to dinner under the maple tree. She holds my hand beneath the table and bends forward to catch every scrap of conversation. Her face lights up when her friends smile, and when they laugh, she joins in. If her laughter is sometimes a beat late, no one seems to notice. She says little beyond Yes and No in answer to questions, but the guests seem relaxed in her company.

Al Jackman, the pharmacist, takes me aside as he leaves

and says, almost angrily, 'I've known your mother all my life. There's nothing wrong with her.'

'Al,' I say, 'she doesn't have the faintest idea who you are.' When he and his wife leave, mother is so tired by the effort she has made that she falls sound asleep within seconds of her head hitting the pillow.

In public, her façade is still intact. With enormous effort, she puts her old personality on public show. In private however, the façade is giving way.

'Where we are now? Is this our house?'

'Yes.'

'Where is our house?'

'It's here. This is your place, and Dad is coming back soon.'

She gives me a wily look, as if she has just caught me lying.

I repeat: 'Hold my hand. I'm here. I'm your son. As long as you're with me, you're going to be OK.'

'I know.' This is precisely what she doesn't know.

Logically, she should give up. The questions are pointless, since she can't remember the answers. Yet all day long we ring the bells, over and over, in the same sequence, as if some region of her mind still believes that simple repetition might just imprint the melody in her mind.

Everything depends on keeping to a routine. Otherwise she becomes agitated and upset. At bedtime, I give her the two green sleeping pills. Then I help her out of her bra and her slip, roll down her tights and slip the nightie over her head. In order to prevent her getting up and trying to put her clothes on again, I put on my pyjamas and get into bed next to her. Even two years ago, her bedside table was still piled high with books. My own love of books comes from her, whereas he regarded literature as a frivolous female amusement park. Now we are down to a single murder mystery. I ask her to read a page to me, and she does so in a childlike singsong, without inflection, unaware that the words are forming into meanings. After a paragraph she stops and puts the book away. Then we lie side by side, staring up at the ceiling, until the evenness of her breathing convinces me she is asleep. Only then do I begin to feel free.

She often wakes in the night and begins to dress hurriedly. I do not try to stop her. She steals downstairs and sits in the dark, clutching her handbag. Who she is waiting for, what she is waiting for, she cannot say. When I come down to breakfast, she is often there, on the downstairs sofa, staring straight ahead.

In the morning, I lever her into the bath, pressing her arms and legs down to make the movements they no longer make on their own. This often amuses her, as if she sees how ridiculous it is for a middle-aged man to be manhandling a naked woman of sixty into a bath. It is as if her mind is miles away from her body, looking down on its ruin and absurdity.

When I bathe her, I remember how she was when I was a child in the changing room of the Alton pool, wiggling out of her one piece, picking it up off the floor with a flick of her toe and then striding to and fro, her underwear in one hand, talking and enclosing me in the secrets of female space. Now as I work the sponge across the knotted muscles of her shoulders, I see her collarbone, the line of her backbone and her ribs beneath her white flesh. When I wash her hair, I feel the contours of her skull beneath my fingers.

I help her from the bath, dry her legs, swathe her in towels, sit her on the edge of the bath and manicure her toenails: they are horny and yellow and her feet are gnarled. She has walked a long way.

As a child, I used to sit with her in the kitchen while she

applied hot depilatory wax to her legs and upper lip with a little brush. She wore a light print dress and drank beer from a bottle. When the wax set, she peeled it off, cursing and wincing and handed me the strips, imbedded with fine black hairs. When it was over, her legs were smooth and silky to the touch.

Now I am shaving those legs with my razor, while she sits perfectly still, smiling at me as if these are not her legs at all. We are very close, her in a towel, me on my knees at her feet, as close as we were when I was a child.

She never complains. The old dignities bred in the bone continue to endure. When we walk up the hill behind the house, I feel her going slower and slower, but she never stops until I do. I ask her whether she is sad, and she says, with more puzzlement than regret, 'It's supposed to be more fun than this.'

And then the questions resume.

'What is going to happen?'

'I told you. Dad returns on Monday.'

'Could you write that down?'

So I write it down in large letters and she folds it in her cardigan pocket and pats it there and says she feels better. Half an hour later, she is waving the paper in front of my face. 'What do I do about this?'

'Nothing. It just tells you what is going to happen.'

'But I didn't know anything of this.'

'Now you do.' I take the paper from her hands and tear it up. It makes no sense to get angry at her, but I do. Sometimes I get angry because I suspect, crazy as it may seem, that she is having me on. Her absences can be uncanny. Sometimes it is as if she has decided to take a vacation from me. At other times, it is as if she has just given up. Either way, she occasionally stares at me with a sly, infuriating expression which says, 'You don't understand, do you?'

As Father's absence lengthens, I lose my temper with her again and again. One night, she fails yet again to set the table properly. I shove her aside, slam the knives and forks into their proper place and hiss, 'Try Mother, try. For Christ's sake.' I badly need something to believe in. I badly need her to give me courage.

If I am angry, so is she. Anger is there in abundance, just below the smudged demeanour she presents to the world. My father has been struck several times, and though she has never struck me, she has come close. I am wary with her when taking off her clothes. You never know when she might recall how undignified it is to be undressed by her own son.

She is ageing at a terrifying rate. There is nothing graceful or gentle about it. Everything is accelerated, like those ghastly time-lapse films of flowers pushing through the soil, flowering and dying in a single moment. She rushes through every moment of the day, like someone possessed, like someone saying, Let's get this damned thing over with. She bolts down her meals, leaps up to clear away the plates before Jack or I have finished.

'What's the hurry?' I ask her.

'I don't know,' she says. She downs whatever I put in her glass. 'You'll enjoy it more if you sip it gently,' I say.

'What a good idea,' she says and then empties the glass with a gulp.

We are on the porch, after dinner, silently watching the car lights through the pine trees at the bottom of the field. She suddenly says, 'I am alone,' not piteously, but in the unemotional voice she used of old when facing up to disagreeable realities.

My wife once said, 'Don't be hard on yourself. She

doesn't feel a thing. The illness takes care of everything. It's worse for you.' Nothing could be farther from the truth. I know she has insight. I know she has counted up every one of her losses. She looks at herself and asks what kind of person she is becoming. The illness spares her nothing.

Every morning she wakes up a little farther away from us. Yet she still manages to convey something, if only with a glance, of the world she is entering. Beyond the fear and the loss, she seems to say, there is life of a sort here, at the dark edge where everything is crumbling, falling away, becoming indistinct. Occasionally her pacing ceases, her hunted look is conjured away by the stillness at dusk, and she sits on the porch, watching the sunlight stream through all the trees they planted over twenty-five years, and I see something pass over her face that I might call serenity, if I believed there was such a thing.

Sometimes at night, lying by her side, I think about all the memory that must remain inside her, trapped within the circuits, denied speech yet still present in her mind. She is the silent custodian of the shadow zone of my own life. She is the only one who can tell me what I was like before I began to remember, the only one who can decipher those first senseless scenes when memory begins. Only she can tell me whose knee I am sitting on, whose hands are steadying me from behind as I lift the blue spun beer glass and cover my face, so that I stare up momentarily into a blue-spun universe that smells of hops. Lying there beside me, she cannot speak, but I know that blue spun glass is somewhere within her, a trapped neural impulse, an infinitesimal synaptic spark in the circuitry of her mind.

I lie beside her, listening as her breathing descends into the rhythm of sleep. Quietly, the thought steals over me. Quietly it takes me over. How easily, how mercifully, how quickly it could all be done. One pillow held over her face for long enough. There is no one to stop me, no one to know. Two minutes is all, and enough pressure. No one would blame me. I am sure I could manage it if I did not have to see her eyes staring up into mine. I lie there debating whether I have the right to save her, whether I have what it takes. My eyes are open. I am lucid and as cold as a stone. Then I realise she is not sleeping but awake beside me, as if she had been listening to my innermost thoughts. Her face against the pillow is like Nettie's now; her blue-grey eyes open in the darkness and beyond all illusion, the blonde braid curled against her neck now feathery white, her cheeks bruised and worn by time, her nightgown buttoned at her neck like a girl's. I want to whisper her name, but I cannot.

I ONCE SAW A television documentary about the neurologist and surgeon, Wilder Penfield, in which he opened the top of a woman's skull under local anaesthetic, exposing the glistening surfaces of her brain. He applied an electrical stimulus to a portion of her hippocampus, and the patient began talking in a low, faraway voice about an afternoon when she and her sister were on a garden swing and one of their feet caught their mother's tea set and sent it flying through the air onto the grass. It seemed wonderful that in the palpitating square of a woman's flesh was memory, the thing itself, the source of that disembodied whisper.

Penfield's experiments, conducted in the 1940s and '50s, appeared to prove that memory functions were localised in different segments of the brain. Procedural memory – the combination of skills necessary for riding a bicycle, for example – was held to be stored in one place; perceptual memory – what home looks like – was stored in another fold of tissue. How did neurologists know this? Because there were people who could still ride a bike, but couldn't remember the way home.

Localisation of function also implied that the memory images stored in different parts of the brain were activated every time recollection occurred. This theory, which Penfield's experiments appeared to confirm, was surely the origin of my belief that my mother's memories were still intact, like a butterfly collection left behind in the attic of an abandoned house.

I began to think that there was something wrong with the idea that her memories were localised and that illness was obliterating them one by one. It was not that she was forgetting discrete events; she was unable to place herself in a meaningful sequence of those events. She knew who she once had been, but not who she had become. Her memories of childhood were intact, but her short-term recollection had collapsed, so that past and present were marooned far from each other.

I suspected that the breakdown in her memory was a symptom of a larger disruption in her ability to create and sustain a coherent image of herself over time. It dawned on me that her condition offered me an unrepeatable opportunity to observe the relation between selfhood and memory. I began to think of my mother as a philosophical problem.

My mistake had been to suppose that a memory image could subsist apart from an image of the self, that memories could persist apart from the act of speaking or thinking about them from a given standpoint. It was this junction between past and present that she was losing. She was wondering who the 'I' was in her own sentences. She was wondering whether these memories of a blue beer mug in a warm suburban garden were really her own. Because they no longer seemed to be her own, she began to throw them away.

In spite of this, her gestures, her smile, her voice remained unchanged. A blurred version of her charm survived, together with hints of her sense of humour. She was suffering a disturbance of her soul, not just a loss of memory, yet *she* was still intact. I was back where I started.

My difficulties in understanding her were not made any easier by the jargon doctors used to describe her condition. What in my childhood had been called 'hardening of the arteries of the brain' was now called 'premature senile dementia'. The one was as absurd as the other. My mother was disturbed but she was anything but senile. Then the doctors took to calling her condition a disease. This at least had the merit of conferring clinical interest upon what, until then, had simply been regarded as the demented confusions of the elderly. When post-mortem examinations of these patients revealed a characteristic pattern of scar tissues in the neural fibres, doctors suddenly believed they had a clinical mystery to unravel.

However the more that doctors discovered, the more puzzling the disease became. While the tangles and plaques – the scar tissue – did obstruct the neurochemical transmission of electrical messages in the brain, they also showed up in alert people whose symptoms were confined to the mild memory loss associated with normal ageing. Some experts weren't even sure whether the scars were a cause or consequence of the forgetting.

'I told you,' my brother said. 'There's a lot we don't know.'

'You don't tell the patients that.'

'I'm telling you. We're not there yet.'

And what about the interaction of heredity and environment? Some authorities maintained that clear evidence of genetic transmission was evident only in early onset cases. Others insisted that genetics was also the dominant factor in late onset cases like my mother's.

My brother must have got tired of fielding my questions and so he arranged for us to meet the big specialist in the city. I couldn't see why we were bothering, and I told him so.

'Don't you want to know?' he said.

'Know what?'

'Where we are. How much time there is.'

'Do you?'

Besides, I said, neurological investigations are humiliating. 'Urine samples, blood samples, X-rays, CAT scans, PET scans. Christ, what do we need this for?'

And so it proved. Mother was led, naked and uncomprehending, into a tiled room and sealed inside a machine that resembled one of those iron lungs in a B-movie. I stood in the control room, on the other side of the glass, watching her terrified glances as her head was placed inside an instrument to measure cerebral activity. Like a fool, I began to wave, though she couldn't see me. Her legs made small, struggling gestures of fear and a technician flicked on the intercom and told her not to. I stood there, beyond the glass, wanting to kill my brother for putting her through this. Then the sedation took hold and she lay awake but motionless, while a stream of images of the neurochemical activity within her brain flowed across the monitors in the control room. The technicians were talkative. They told me what to look for: bright blue for the skull casing, red for the cerebral lobes, purple for the tracer. I stood there watching brightly coloured neural images of Mother's fear and dread.

Three weeks later, we are all sitting in the neurologist's office getting the results, my father, my brother, my mother and I. The doctor is a fashionable middle-aged woman who happens to be a paraplegic in a wheelchair. Beneath her desk I can see her withered legs in a pair of smart black stockings and buckled shoes. With guilty goodwill, I think here at last is someone who will understand.

Looking over the top of her bifocals, she says with a warm smile,

'How are we today?'

Mother says, 'We are fine today.'

'Good, good,' replies the doctor.

'So what's the situation?' my father asks, looking up from his hands.

The doctor smooths open the clinical file. 'Mother,' she says, 'is performing pretty well on some tests, not quite so well on others.'

It doesn't seem right to be talking about her in the third person when she is in the room. I glare at my brother, who rises and escorts Mother out. My brother and the doctor exchange a nod as Mother makes her laboured transit to the door.

When the door shuts behind her, the doctor resumes. 'The scans are confirming what you already know,' and here she gestures at the reports. 'Discernible shrinkage of the cerebellum, reduction in size and volume of hippocampus, possible evidence of cerebral trauma.'

At the word trauma, my father raises his eyes. 'Must be the car accident.'

'Tell me about that,' she says, taking up a pen. In the shattered silence after impact, I see my father's bloody face lying against the steering wheel and my mother's broken body slumped beside him. Words are resounding in my head, my brother is looking at me, his hands at his temples, blood streaming through his fingers.

The doctor says head trauma, in road accident victims and in boxers, can produce amnesias of Mother's sort. So head trauma is pencilled into her list of causative factors, beside heredity, environment, exposure to neuro-toxins. She says the more causes that can be enumerated, the more we are likely to understand. Actually, it seems to me, the more causes you can identify, the more mysterious her condition becomes; but I decide not to argue the point. 'Of course,' she goes on, 'the gold standard for all diagnosis in these cases is . . . '

'Autopsy,' I butt in.

A thought crosses her mind.

'So you know about these things?' she says, brightly. I nod and I don't know whether she is marking me down as one of those tedious neurological autodidacts or as a mature professional she can take into her confidence. Whatever she thinks, she knows I will be doing the talking. My father has withdrawn into a cave of silence.

I ask her the prognosis. She looks at my father's bent head and says, in a softer voice than before, 'Your wife will be dead in three years.'

My father sits with his hands on his knees as if steadying himself.

'I'm sorry,' she says.

She takes my father through the entire *via dolorosa* ahead: which function will break down when, how soon she will cease to recognise us, how soon epilepsy is likely to set in. There is no doubt that she believes such candour is a way of treating us with respect, and I feel grateful for it, but I keep thinking there must be some mistake. 'But each case is different.'

'There are recurrent features,' she begins.

'I mean, in some early onset cases, you do die in three years, but in late onset cases, the process can take longer, surely . . . '

She looks down at the papers on her desk. 'I'm looking at these scans.'

I shift tack. 'I used to think she was just falling apart. Now I think she has developed strategies of her own for dealing with this.'

The doctor nods. I see her place her hand on her knee and shift her inert leg and its fashionable shoe.

'Take the business about her language,' I say. 'She can't maintain a conversation, but the way she listens, and laughs when you say something that amuses her, nods to let you know she's following what you say.'

The doctor seems interested. 'Her semantic and syntactic memory functions have collapsed, but prosodic variation is still intact.'

'Prosodic variation?'

She means tone of voice, facial expression, gestures. Some patients begin to drawl or stutter in a voice they have never used before. 'They hear themselves speak,' she says, 'and they think who is this?'

'That's not Mother. She still knows who she is. She may not talk correctly, but she's still able to take part in a conversation. She still has her social skills.'

The doctor is good-naturedly persistent. 'Her prosodic variation is still intact.'

It is the word 'still' that bothers me.

'You keep telling me what has been lost, and I keep telling you something remains.'

'I just see what I see. From the clinical point of view,' the doctor says, looking at me over the tops of her bifocals. There is something admirable about this candour, about this refusal to indulge my hopes. Much against my will, I can't help but like her, though I can tell we see my mother so differently that there is no middle ground between us.

I want to say that my mother's true self remains intact, there at the surface of her being, like a feather resting on the surface tension of a glass of water, in the way she listens, nods, rests her hand on her cheek, when we are together. But I stumble along and just stop.

The doctor tries to help me out. 'This seems to matter to you.'

'Because,' I say, 'a lot depends on whether people like you treat her as a human being or not.'

She is too clever to rise to this. She deals with beleaguered and hostile relatives all the time. 'This is difficult for you. I know that. My job is to give you the facts.'

I wonder what my brother has told her about me, and why they both feel certain I need such an astringent dose of reality therapy. I change tack again. 'It's important not to humour her.'

'I never humour anyone.'

'She has to believe we understand her. Otherwise she'll just give up.'

'*Do* you understand?'

'Sometimes, sometimes not.'

'Well, isn't that humouring her?' she parries.

'So I pretend,' I reply. 'She needs respect,' I say, unsure why I am saying it.

'Of course.' And then she says, reflectively, 'Though who knows what respect means.'

'Just giving her the benefit of the doubt. Just assuming there might be some method in the madness.'

The doctor smiles. 'So act "as if" she is rational. Behave "as if" she knows what she is saying.'

'Exactly.'

I tell her how Mother goes in and out of the bathroom five times an hour. Because she does not want to wet herself but can't tell when she last went to the bathroom. So her strategy is to behave 'as if' she needs to go to the bathroom, whenever the thought occurs to her. There is a method here. This is not just random, panic-stricken behaviour. Self-respect is in play here. This is how she manages to avoid making a mess of herself. My voice rises at this point and both of us go silent.

'From a clinical point of view,' she says, taking up the thread, 'disinhibition begins with disintegration in the frontal lobes. Your mother's frontal lobes are not yet affected,' the neurologist goes on, 'which would help to explain why she is continent and why she is gentle.'

'She's gentle,' I say, 'because that's the kind of person she is.'

'I know how you must feel.'

'Besides,' I say, 'disinhibition is an ugly word.'

'I know,' she said, with a nod in the direction of the hospital wards somewhere down the corridor. Those wards are brimful of disinhibition. It is this doctor's life.

'Disinhibition suggests everything is just beyond her. Actually, she is struggling.'

The neurologist looks at me evenly, as if debating whether to despatch this illusion as well. She must have heard it from relatives a thousand times before. She decides to say nothing. It doesn't matter. I change tack once more.

'You sound like my brother.'

'I'll take that as a compliment,' she said.

'I mean it.' Our smiles declare a truce.

It is pointless to go on and we both know it. The doctor looks at Mother's PET scans and sees a disease of memory function, with a stable name and a clear prognosis. I see an illness of selfhood, without a name or even a clear cause.

My father is becoming restive, as if wishing to remind us that we are arguing about his wife.

The doctor reaches into a drawer in her desk and takes out a form. She fills in something at the top and then passes it across the desk to my father.

'I would like to include your wife in our study. The clinical picture she presents will be of great interest to us.' She touches the form with a red fingernail. 'I'll need your consent on her behalf.'

'Consent for what?'

'To allow us to remove her brain following autopsy for special study here at the clinic.'

My father looks down at his hands for a moment and then, drawing in his breath like someone about to lift a heavy load, raises himself to his full height. He picks the paper off the desk and flicks it back at her with a brisk gesture of contempt. Then he strides out of the room.

I BEGAN PAYING MORE attention to books which I used to despise: the health and personal growth books, always shelved next to psychology and the occult. I began buying paperbacks with titles like: *You Can Beat Cancer in Sixty Steps*, *The Power Immune Diet*, *Love Yourself and Live*, *Super Immunity*, *Say Yes to Life* and so on. These books popularise the findings of a new branch of medicine called 'psychoneuroimmunology', which studies the relation between mental and emotional states and the body's immune system. They argue that a positive mental attitude can retard or reverse the course of illness. Mind over matter. Soul over body. Spirit over cell decay.

On the phone, my brother was so scornful about these books that I asked him whether he had actually read any of them. He sighed, 'Life is too short.'

'Actually,' I said, 'they're pretty interesting.'

'For God's sake.'

'Well,' I said, 'if you had cancer and someone came along and said, "if you have positive mental attitude, you can beat this thing," you would try it.'

'I'd try anything. But believing is another matter,' he said.

'That's just like you,' I said.

'What do you mean?'

'Forget it,' I said.

Now that the doctor had left us in no doubt about what was in store, I hated, with all my heart, the idea that there was nothing any of us could do. I thought I detected instances where Mother had been able, through great force of will, to cup her hands round a thought to keep it from running through her fingers. I longed to believe that she was holding back the force of illness with the power of her will. But I wondered whether I wasn't deluding myself.

My wife's view was that I was becoming too obsessed to see anything clearly, but I said it felt righteous to be obsessed. As if appraising me from a great distance, she said 'You have children, remember? They're growing up. Every day they're different. But you wouldn't know. You've spent the last seven weekends up at the farm.'

I couldn't deny this either, but the inference – that I didn't care about my children – was ridiculous, and I said so. By bringing the children into it, she seemed to be implying that I was choosing my mother over my children, the dying over the living. Or maybe that's just my idea. I didn't really know what she thought, and at the time, I didn't care.

She thought the illness was taking me over, while I felt I was struggling to work myself free. Why else was I reading these books about 'positive mental attitude'? I didn't need my brother to tell me they were shallow. That was what I found touching about them. These books wanted to believe something. So did I. The problem was that I knew too much for my own good. After all, I taught philosophy to undergraduates for a living. It always takes time to realise what a profession does to you, how it grinds down the innocent hopefulness you start your life with. Philosophy does this more than most careers: it tests innocence and faith to destruction. I loved my discipline and respected it, perhaps too much. I now see that I should have worried more about being disillusioned and less about being naïve. At the time, I mistook my disillusion for a form of wisdom.

Certainly it appeared more adult than faith, especially the bug-eyed kind of faith displayed in these books.

This is by way of explaining why, when I came to write an essay about these self-help books, I was scathing, despite what I had said to my brother on the phone. I took the naïve credulity in these books and did what a philosopher is paid to do: I snuffed it out.

What is more, I gave a lecture on the subject. And not just to my college class, but to the Alton Rotarians, at their Friday night discussion meeting in the community hall. The reasons for doing so were obvious. My father had given a lecture there. So had my brother. At last my turn had come. More than eighty people turned up, and my wife brought along my mother and father.

The lecture was called 'Illness and Stoicism'.

> In *Thus Spake Zarathustra*, Nietzsche imagined a future race of beings whom he called 'the last men'. Nietzsche said of them: 'they have their little pleasure by day and their little pleasure for the night: but they respect health.'
>
> Nietzsche could see them jogging toward him: bright-faced creatures in their tracksuits, hearts beating, lungs dilating, heads brimming with the music on their Walkmen. These last men and women, he predicted, would convert sex into recreation; religion into athletics; introspection into positive thinking; and the human good – in all its tragic complexity – to the glow of physical well-being. The gyms, squash courts, Nautilus rooms, swimming lanes and saunas of the big cities resound with the thud and grunt of the last men and women. North Americans commonly list health at the top of their preoccupations, ahead of love, work or money.

Health is a dawn to dusk regimen, with plenty of bedside reading. Books on health have displaced books on philosophy as sources of edification. The American self-help tradition of Horatio Alger, Mary Baker Eddy and Norman Vincent Peale now talks the language of immunology, biofeedback and stress management.

Yet if the health books are anything to go by, the rat race is as hard on the winners as it is on the losers. The new books on health warn that American striving can be lethal. The American corporate ideal of the competitive over-achiever is nothing other than a heart attack waiting to happen. The killer instincts of the business class are killing off the killers.

Health has replaced ethical scruple as the limiting ideology of a predatory business culture. Zarathustra's 'last men' have long since drawn back from capitalism red in tooth and claw. 'They have left the places where living was hard: for one needs warmth. One still loves one's neighbour and rubs oneself against him: for one needs warmth.'

The latest trend catering to the health anxieties of the American commercial class is psychoneuroimmunology, the science that studies the feedback mechanisms between psychological states of mind and the body's immune system. Chronic stress, for example, causes the adrenal glands to pump chemicals into the bloodstream which inhibit the immune function. Conversely, immune activity in the body's hormones may 'talk back' to the brain's neurotransmitters, causing changes in states of mind. This research confirms what holistic healers have always preached: that patients with a strong will to live and a supportive social network are likely to survive traumatic illness better than those who are fatalistic and alone.

There is an elective affinity between an immunology which asserts that patients can cure themselves and an American cultural credo which insists that the individual is master of his or her destiny. The new immunology is the bearer of an arduous style of moral Prometheanism. It tells us, once again, that man's will shall make him master of his fate.

Prometheanism is noble but it is hell on the weak. The upbeat message of the new American psychology of health may be: you can cure yourself. The downbeat message is: if treatment fails you have only yourself to blame. The modern route to health means mobilising immense resources of self-regard. What about all those normal souls who don't happen to adore themselves?

Not for the last men the health-giving virtues of irony, or the wisdom of Nietzsche's remark: 'the time of the most contemptible man is coming, the man who can no longer despise himself.' Self-contempt, in the new dispensation, is merely a negative mental attitude, an invitation to a heart attack, open house for a tumour.

Beyond the implausible degree of self-regard required by the new regime of positive mental attitude, there is an obvious contradiction at the heart of it. It is one thing to argue that distress or low mental states can *affect* immunological responsiveness: there is a sound medical basis for such views. But it is quite another to say that emotions *cause* disease. Still another to believe that a positive mental attitude can reverse biological processes. Of course mental attitude matters. Diseases whose cures have been found become mere diseases; those we do not yet understand become metaphorical carriers of everything we fear and loathe.

We should try, Susan Sontag writes, to 'regard cancer as if it were just a disease, a very serious one, but just a disease. Not a curse, not a punishment, not an embarrassment. Without "meaning". And not necessarily a death sentence.'

Living an illness without giving it 'meaning' would seem to require us to be as individualistic as we can, refusing to succumb to the contagion of fear which sweeps through everyone when we learn that we are ill. Living without metaphor also means trusting the doctor, because only medicine approaches disease non-metaphorically.

The obstacles to such trust, however, remain enormous. The problem is how to build a relation between doctor and patient in which real individuals can exchange understandings, rather than re-enact the symbolic roles of parent and child. Crucial to this relation is a shared appreciation of the limited purchase of medicine upon fate.

What is needed is a shared stoicism, in which patient and doctor reach an understanding of what medicine can and cannot do. Stoicism, not surprisingly, is an ideal in retreat in the modern world. Now that so much illness has been conquered, stoic acceptance of biological fate is equated with fatalism. Suffer and be still no longer. The 'last men' of modernity have junked the culture of endurance for the sake of a culture of complaint. They go into illness as rights bearers, as vigilant bundles of informed consent. The stoic tradition, on the other hand, did address itself to a question the culture of complaint cannot answer: when should I struggle and when should I give in?

All moral behaviour proceeds by metaphor. Some of it is pernicious, some of it is useful. How do we tell which is which? It is good, I think, to wish to think of patients as struggling agents in some degree responsible for their reaction to the experience of illness. Struggling may even improve their chances of survival. We do need to feel we are responsible. We need to feel that we are adequate to our fate, that we have not been found wanting.

Yet we must not think badly of persons who despair, who feel terror or horror at their own disintegration. It is easier to praise stoic courage, than it is to admire terror, but we owe respect to both.

The real problem, of course, is what we are to think of death. People like us who live by the values of self-mastery are not especially good at dying, at submitting to biological destiny. The modern problem is not death without religious consolation, without an afterlife. The problem is that death makes the modern secular religion of self-development and self-improvement appear senseless. We are addicted to a vision of life as narrative, which we compose as we go along. In fact, we didn't have anything to do with the beginning of the story; we are merely allowed to dabble with the middle; and the end is mostly not up to us at all, but to genetics, biological fate and chance. Accepting death would mean giving up on the metaphor of life as narrative. Accepting illness would mean living ironically, accepting that we go into battle against biological fate as underdogs. We can struggle, but we are likely to lose.

There was polite applause at the end, and afterwards, when people were filing out, Al Jackman came up, with his hat in his hands, and said it was pretty strong stuff as far as he was concerned. By the look on his face, I could see he meant it was more than he cared to think about, and I thought, as a young philosophy teacher might, that it was a good thing to make Al Jackman feel uncomfortable. Friends and neighbours were making their way through the centre aisle to the steps down to the parking lot. Outside car wheels began turning on the gravel and the low beams flashed into the hall. My father and mother came towards me, holding hands, an old, diminished couple in a thinning crowd. I wanted to feel I had reached them, for I had been talking to no one else. Father patted my elbow and then let his hand fall back into hers.

'Difficult matters. Very difficult.' He was trying to find something good to say. He knew he mustn't let me down, so he smiled, uneasily, as if at war with himself and tried to make a joke. 'Alton has many worried Rotarians tonight.'

Mother stood a little to one side, looking down at the bare floorboards and the rows of vacant aluminium chairs. Suddenly she tugged my father's hand and said in a firm voice, 'I want to go home now.' Then, without so much as looking at me, she walked out. I turned to my wife.

'What was that all about?' I said.

'Don't you know?' my wife replied.

'As it happens, I don't.'

'You were talking about her death.'

'I was talking about my own death, not hers.'

'I don't care what you thought you were doing. Think about what it sounded like to her. You were saying to her, "You are going to struggle, and it won't make all that much difference because you are going to die, and all of us are going to have to accept that." '

'If I was saying that, how do you know she understood?'

'It's a reasonable supposition.'

'What's wrong with it anyway?'

'Well, it isn't a message any one of us particularly wants to hear in front of eighty people in a public hall. If you've got something to say, why don't you just say it to her face.' And with that, she turned and walked down the aisle and out into the parking lot. I walked home alone, down Main Street, beneath the yellow blinking light at the crossroads with Atwater, and I felt that every shuttered shop window, every fenced garden was barred against me.

THE SUMMER AFTER that lecture, I took Jack up to the farm to spend a week with my parents. When I told my wife I was going, she looked so exasperated I said that they were my family and I had to be there.

'We're your family, you fool,' she said.

We had got beyond argument, so I slammed the front door behind me and got into the car. Jack was in the back seat and I muttered, 'I don't know why she doesn't understand.' Jack looked back at the house and then at me and said nothing. I see him in the mirror, staring at me as he was when I drove away that morning, his face tight and closed against me.

Our daughter had made a necklace for my mother, and I promised to deliver it. It was made of coloured beads in a pattern that looked haphazard to me but not to my daughter. As she strung it together, she muttered, 'One little one, one big one, one round one, one square one, one little one' and so on until it was long enough, and she then said, 'There. For Granny.'

I wasn't sure I could give it to my mother. She had torn off one necklace already, when my father had tried to place one round her neck, and she did the same when he tried to pin a brooch to her lapel. She had pushed him away and stalked off to the other end of the room, looking cornered and angry. This hurt my father but he understood that she resented our presumption that we could adorn her as we wished. 'She is not a Christmas tree after all,' he said.

This time, instead of placing it round her neck, I laid it in her hands and explained who had made it. She turned the necklace over and felt each bead with her fingers, as if trying to figure out the logic of my daughter's pattern. Then she slipped the necklace over her head and smiled shyly. Father gave her a hug. 'Aren't you looking pretty, girl.'

'I'm not a girl,' my mother said with slow deliberation.

Mother was beginning to spill things by then, so to keep her neat and clean, my father had changed her wardrobe, substituting bright, easy to wash nylon skirts and blouses for the more costly and subtle clothes my mother used to wear. The trouble was, and you couldn't explain this to Father, the new clothes made Mother look like the inmate of a nursing home. Now as I took her over to the mirror in the downstairs hallway and placed her where she could see herself, she gazed at her weather-beaten face, at the alien Terylene frock and the child's necklace and she said, softly, 'Old. Very old.'

At dinner, my father, in his apron, ladelled the soup into four bowls and we ate in silence, broken only by the sound of my parents chewing their bread and swallowing their soup. Then I began talking for the sake of talking; about college politics and baseball and anything I could think of, just to keep them entertained. In other words, it was Showtime, and I was in the middle of it, when Mother got up from the table and began pacing about the room, ignoring me. She muttered something, but I could not make out what it was. She came back to the table and took her soupbowl into the kitchen. Then she went upstairs, and we could hear her walking about. When she came downstairs again, my father said, 'Oh do sit down, dear, for God's sake.' My mother came over to the table and as she sat down, Father tried to take her hand, but she pulled it away and stared fixedly at him, her face a mixture of misery and loathing, such as I had never seen before.

I took her upstairs as soon as was decent and helped her to undress. I lifted the necklace off her neck and she made a particular point of laying it on top of her clothes on the chair. When she was in bed, I sat beside her and smoothed the covers and made idle conversation to pass the minutes before the sedation took hold. To humour her, I pointed to her painting of the headland at Antigonish which hung on the wall of the bedroom facing her. Pointing at the storm clouds which she had painted over the headland, I said, 'The storm is coming.' She raised her eyes coldly to the picture and said, 'Just paint.' Then she turned away from me.

Jack went to bed by himself and my father and I sat up for an hour, watching the late night news on television, to an accompaniment of Father's growls and shakes of his head. That night, Gorbachev had promised to free prices on foodstuffs and my father muttered, 'That will be the end of him.'

As he said this, sitting in his rocking chair in a pair of old corduroys and bedroom slippers, his face bathed in the light of the television screen, I looked at his old hands on the chair, with the nails bitten down and dirty with soil from the flowerbeds, I thought, for an instant, that I saw him as he was, a grain merchant's son from Odessa who had travelled a long way from home. He leaned forward and snapped off the television and then we sat together in silence. I asked him how he was feeling, and he rubbed his chest in an absent gesture and said he was fine, just fine. He stroked the top of his right hand with his left, and said, not looking at me, but gazing at the floor, 'She's left me now. I wish I could go with her.' He glanced at me, for a second, just to let me know how it was and that he was prepared for whatever was in store. I couldn't think of anything to say and so we sat for a few more minutes in near darkness.

'Goodnight, boy.'

'Goodnight.'

I awoke at about four in the morning to sounds coming from their room next door. A chair was scraped along the bare boards of their room and a body bumped against the wall. I heard something like a scuffle and raised voices. Then I heard her venture out onto the landing and begin descending the stairs. My father came out of their bedroom and I heard him say, 'I didn't mean it, please.' And then, 'Come back to bed, darling, do.' I put on a dressing gown and came out on the landing. By this time they were both downstairs in the hall by the front door.

They were bathed in the faint light cast by the porch lamp At first I thought they were embracing. She had a raincoat on over her nightie and was wearing my daughter's necklace round her neck, and her feet were bare. My father was in his pyjamas and he had his arms round her and his head locked against hers. She was fighting to break free of his grip. Their movements were slow, exhausted and desperate. She thrashed and he tried clumsily to ward her off. 'Don't,' he moaned and she shouted, 'Let me go!' I stood at the top of the stairs, too shocked to move. Then she broke free and grabbed hold of the door handle, frantically turning it this way and that. It opened and she stepped on to the porch. Father lunged for her, grabbed her by the shoulders and pulled her back inside. She pivoted within his grasp, raised her arms and began to strike at him, while he shrank back and tried to maintain his hold. At this moment, as I took another step forward, my daughter's necklace suddenly snapped. The wooden beads slipped from the broken string and cascaded to the floor below, scattering across the hall into every corner of the sitting room behind. All you could hear was the beads bouncing and rolling out of sight on the hardwood floor. Like two figures in a tragedy, watching the vanishing order of their world collapse round them, they stood stock-still staring at their hands in recognition of what they had done. Then she fell to her knees with a groan and he followed, and they both began scrabbling about, trying frantically to recover the beads which were still rolling away from their reach. Too late to stop them, too late to lift them up, I stood on the stairs watching my parents sobbing on all fours in the dark.

I DO NOT KNOW how to proceed with the story and I even wonder why it is that I am telling it as a story. For the next afternoon, my father died. I want to describe how it happened, but I can't understand the force of my own desire to do so. Why exactly does anyone want to retell an experience of that sort? What is this, a compulsion to confess? Confess to whom? Confess what?

I do not need the catharsis. I accept his death. But wait. Accept, accept, what does the word mean? Who alive can ever know what it would mean to accept death? Telling the story of any death is a way to pretend that you have mastered it, that you have accepted and come to terms with it. It is a lie you tell yourself to keep going. You say, 'This is how it happened. First this, then this, then that.' As if the storyteller is the puppeteer, when as it happens, as the impossible and unthinkable thing occurs, it is you who dance to the jerking of the strings.

So I cannot pretend otherwise. I do not accept it. Or feel reconciled to it. I merely feel tired of it, and that in itself is the best reason to tell the story again. With time, the sharpness of that day has faded. Year by year, the pain has leached away so that now I sometimes wonder whether I remain capable of feeling anything about him. Tell the story, then, to recover yourself, to recover him. Tell the story so that his death finally happens.

At breakfast that morning, my father cupped his hand

around his coffee and looked out across the fields. He ignored the beads which were in a bowl on the table between us. Then he passed his hand over his forehead and laughed. 'What a mess, eh boy? What a mess.'

He went upstairs and began running her bath. When I passed by the bedroom, I heard him say, 'Come on, darling, let's get you washed.'

'I don't want a bath.'

'Every morning, that's the routine. Come on.'

He helped her into the bath and sat on the toilet seat, holding her hand, as he always did, while she dozed in the water. Then he lifted her out, towelled her down, helped her to dress and turned her over to me for the day. He disappeared into his study to finish a review. A couple of times, from behind the door, I heard him swear and once he banged the table with his fist. This was usually a good sign, almost as good as when he whistled.

I can't remember everything I did that day. I walked her down to the postbox at the end of the drive to pick up the mail and back again, made her egg-mayonnaise sandwiches for lunch, took her upstairs for a nap. After that, I walked up the hill behind the house with my son, and we lined up tin cans on a fence post and then I showed him how to blow them away with my 22.

At four that afternoon, while my mother was asleep upstairs, Father came down with a manila envelope and asked me to take it into town and mail it at the post-office. Jack said he wanted to go too and we decided to walk. At the gate I glanced back at the house and I saw that my father was still there on the porch steps, following us with his eyes.

After I mailed off my father's review, we stopped at the drugstore for a couple of cones and walked home, barefoot and single file on the blacktop, eating maple-pecan ice-cream, both of us cool in the shade of the pines along the side of the road. We stopped by the Nixons' farm and bent over the culvert looking for frogs, but didn't see any.

I was starting up the drive, with Jack straggling along behind me, chewing on a length of spear grass, when I saw my mother striding rapidly towards us down the drive, away from the house, with her head down. For a few seconds she didn't see us. Then she lifted her head, saw us and stood still, like an animal sensing a predator. We were a hundred yards apart, Jack and I by the postbox at the bottom of the drive, and Mother at the top of it, framed between a row of scrub pine. Suddenly, she veered to her right, off the drive and began running clumsily into the orchard, stumbling in the high grass, bending beneath the tree branches, losing her balance, getting up again, falling, rising. I began running and calling her name, but she was in full flight, ducking beneath the low branches, her arms flailing to keep her balance, one shoe left behind now in the grass.

I caught up with her and took her by the shoulders trying to shake the cold stare out of her eyes.

'Don't hurt me,' she said in a broken whisper.

'Mother, Mother,' I called.

With her eyes open wide, she said, 'Why is this happening?'

I shook her again. 'What are you talking about?' I was almost shouting. Then she turned in my arms and waved back in the direction of the house. I looked back, told Jack to hold on to her and I dashed towards the house.

A cup was lying in pieces on the porch amidst a dark splash of liquid, a pair of glasses, one of the lenses jarred loose, had fallen on the gravel and some pages of newspaper were drifting among the flowerbeds. There was a pair of drag marks on the gravel leading from the bottom of the porch steps. He was half kneeling, half-slumped on the foot-high retaining wall in front of the flowerbeds. There was blood coming from a cut on his chin. I fell to my knees and got my weight under him and turned him over so I was sitting on the wall and he was lying with his head in my lap. I wiped the blood off his chin and pulled open his shirt and rubbed his chest. His eyes were closed and his mouth was half-open and his forehead was warm. His brow was slightly furrowed, as if he were puzzled by something. I knew I wasn't going to be able to move him, so I held on to him, to keep him from slipping back onto the gravel. Father, I said. Father. Then my mother was in front of us, holding my son's hand, edging closer, then backing away, her eyes wide, her right hand making as if to push the sight away. I told Jack to get her inside. He pulled her with him and I heard him lock the door and saw him going to the phone by the refrigerator. Through the picture window, I saw him dial and turn to look at me. I rubbed Father's shoulders and arms to keep him warm. His legs were buckled at a bad angle but I couldn't straighten them out. I tried to make him look better, smoothing down the hair on the back of his head and dabbing away more blood from the stubble on his chin. Mother was pacing back and forth behind the picture window, while Jack kept close to her, trying to keep hold of her arm. With my free hand, I waved to him to get her away from the window, but she shook him loose, not taking her eyes off the sight.

I don't know how long I was there before an ambulance man was down on his knees, speaking to me, while another one was lifting Father off my lap and slipping the stretcher under him. I made to climb into the back of the ambulance, but the driver came over and took my arm and led me into the house. When I came into the sitting room, my mother was still at the picture window, with Jack at her side, watching the slow revolving blue light on the roof of the ambulance vanishing among the pines.

I got Mother upstairs, undressed her and put her to bed. I sat with her for a while, and I held her hand till she settled. She stared up at the ceiling, then at me, then at the ceiling, then her wide, alarmed eyes began to close. Jack watched from the doorway.

After they phoned from the hospital, I came downstairs and lay down on the sofa. Jack lay down beside me. His hair smelled like hay and I held on to him and felt I was falling over and over in the darkness.

I hadn't been fooled by anything, by the warmth of my father's skin or the puzzled expression on his face. Ten minutes earlier, and I might have got there in time. If I had not eaten that ice-cream, if I had not stopped to talk to Al Jackman at the Drugmart, if we had not got down on our knees to look for frogs in the culvert; if any of these things had not happened, I might have caught him before the cup slid from his hand and his glasses fell off and he hit the gravel on his knees. Ten minutes earlier and he might not have died alone. Ten minutes earlier and he might have known it was me.

When I finished telling my brother this on the phone, there was such a long silence that I spoke his name. Then he said mine. After he had found his usual voice again, he said that the next plane was tomorrow morning and he hung up.

My wife arrived after dark. I put my head on her shoulder and said that I didn't know what to say. 'You don't have to say anything,' she said. Looking into her eyes, I wondered what I must look like. Why was she looking at me like this?

When I thought everybody was asleep, I walked from room to room, turning the lights on and off. His dressing gown hung on the bathroom hook, above the plastic beach shoes he wore about the house. I could still smell his face in the towel by the sink. His typewriter lay open on his writing desk, and there was a page in it. A faded postcard of a Russian saint, the only icon in the house, stared down at me from the top right-hand corner of his study. I just wanted to see myself, finally, as he had seen me, through those hazel eyes. I wanted to believe I had said everything I ever wanted to say to him, and I hoped that he had understood what I had felt, the night before, in front of the television, sitting side by side in the darkened room. But I knew it was too late now. There would always have been more to say.

I went downstairs to get myself a glass of milk and when I came into the kitchen, she was standing in the dark, just outside the kitchen door, looking out at the fields. 'Come on, sweetheart. Inside,' I said, and she turned and let herself be led back into the house, though I couldn't be sure, what with the lateness of the hour and the sedation, that she knew who I was. It didn't matter, we were together. I sat her down at the kitchen table and poured us both a glass of milk. She was in her light blue short-sleeved nightdress and her arms were white and bare. She drank her glass of milk and when she finished there was a trace of milk on her upper lip. I made to wipe it off with a kitchen towel but she pulled her head away She traced a figure on the table with her hand, and I wondered how I was going to tell her. In the event, I didn't have to. She looked at me and whispered, 'I do not have a husband.' She looked down and drew another shape on the table.

AT TWOMEY'S, THE funeral home in Alton, organ music was playing above the hum of an air-conditioner in the room where the coffin lay, on a raised pedestal surrounded by poinsettias. My brother asked Mrs Twomey to turn it off. 'Take as long as you want,' she said when she left us alone. The music stopped with a mechanical click.

My brother sat leaning against the wall in one corner and I sat in another. He stared straight ahead, with his hands on the knees of his blue suit.

I had delivered my father's blazer and white shirt, and they had dressed him in that. The rest of his body was concealed by the coffin. Fred Twomey had rearranged his face the way undertakers do, by working from a photograph and his memory of my father. Most of all, Fred Twomey worked from his general idea of how the dead ought to look: he had taken out Father's dental plate and had invented an expression for him that looked all wrong, ill at ease and embarrassed, as if he were listening to some off-colour story. When I went up to take a closer look, I could see some marks at his right temple and I wondered how they had got there. I was going to reach out and touch his face but I didn't want to remember the chill of death. In fact, I knew I didn't want to remember him this way at all. I walked out and left my brother behind. Half way out of town, he caught up with me in the car, but I waved him on. I wanted to be on my own, to get the sight out of my mind.

When I got back to the house, my wife was fixing my brother a cup of coffee. He pulled a manilla envelope from the funeral home out of his suit pocket and passed it across the kitchen table. Inside were a couple of quarters, a box of matches, some throat lozenges, my father's watch and his wedding ring. I put them all back into the envelope and pushed it towards him. The envelope lay there between us.

Then he said, 'At least she didn't know what happened. We can thank the illness for that.'

I felt all the numbed portions of myself come alive and I said, 'What gives you the right to say what she does and doesn't know?' Then I told him what she had said to me the previous night, sitting at this very table.

'I have my feelings about this too,' he said, after another silence. My wife stood between the two of us, watching.

'You think I don't know that?'

'This is a bad time, we're all going through a bad time.'

'What is this "we" all of a sudden? You haven't been here and you're telling me what "we" feel about every damned thing.'

I felt ashamed of having lost my temper so I got up and slammed the back door. I walked up to the hilltop in the back pasture and sat there on my own, looking at the house, remembering how my wife had said it was like a liner, alone on the night sea, and feeling now that all of us were sinking.

My wife came up after a while and sat down beside me. She picked at the grass at her feet and I put my arm round her shoulder. I was sure that it hadn't just been his heart that had given way. Her illness had killed him. He had enslaved himself to it and when it had finished with him, it had thrown him away.

'He just couldn't do anything more. We all should have helped him, but we didn't know how, and he wouldn't let us, and the result is he's dead. And now my brother comes home and wants me to think that the illness spared her knowing what happened to him. I can't stand it.'

My wife did not try to reason me out of this. She just sat with me until I quietened down, and then when Jack and his sister came out the back door looking for us, she rose to her feet. She rested her hand on my head for an instant and said, 'All I know is you're going to have to stop fighting long enough to bury him.'

We buried him in the municipal cemetery in the next concession road to ours. It was an Episcopalian service, because the Russian priest in the city was away on holiday, and none of us knew the Russian words to perform the service on our own.

When we were children, he used to take us into the city for Russian Easter and Christmas. It was an exile's service, half in English, half in Russian, some of the families attending so North American they could have been with the Baptists across the street, while standing beside old Russian women in kerchiefs, who kneeled to touch their foreheads on the floor. The choir was above and behind you in the balcony, secretaries, clerks and insurance salesmen who stumbled sometimes over the words, as my father did too, forgetting some of the responses, following behind as best he could in a hoarse, ragged bass.

Looking at his coffin in the cemetery on the hillside near our home, I wanted to believe that he had known all along he would end up being buried among strangers, with foreign prayers and that he hadn't expected anything less or wanted anything more. But I wouldn't ever know what he had expected or wanted. He hadn't expected to watch his wife destroyed before his eyes. He hadn't expected to die coming down the porch steps.

A small crowd of townspeople stood some way off, on

the other side of the low iron fence ringing the cemetery. I recognised the couple who did our dry-cleaning and Al Jackman and Hubert Hill from the garage. It was a misty afternoon, with a light breeze across the hilltop. I stood with my mother and my wife and children, and my brother stood to one side, staring at the pebbly brown earth thrown up on either side of our father's casket. The whole service seemed dry and bare, and half of the words were lost in the breeze and it all seemed over before it began. My mother wouldn't go near the grave, so I took my children up and we held hands and we all stared down so that they would see it and never forget it. The clergyman went back to his car and slipped out of his vestments, the crowd dispersed down the hillside and I followed them, leaving my brother alone by the grave side. He didn't come down till an hour later.

It was my wife's idea to take Mother home to our place in the city that night. My wife said she didn't want to spend another night in the house, with all my father's things. Besides, she said the kids had been through enough. At first I didn't agree.

'It's a bad thing to change her routine, especially now.'

My wife looked at me and said quietly, 'There's no routine left.'

That was enough to send me upstairs to pack my mother's things. I waved my family off down the driveway, my mother in the front seat, upright, not looking back at the house where she had spent half her life.

My wife must have intended that my brother and I should be left alone. I made some scrambled eggs and served them with a beer on the kitchen table, but he wouldn't settle. He ate and then stayed in the sitting room on his own. I remained in the kitchen and drank.

Eventually he came in to get another Coors, and as he

opened the refrigerator door, he suddenly said, not to me, but to himself, 'Fathers die every day. A son knows his father is going to die. This is the programme. Since time began. What is this thing we can't speak about? What is this thing that makes us wordless?'

It was as if he was giving a lecture, in a soft voice, to his medical ethics class. Then he slammed the refrigerator door and sat down. 'We are the only animals who don't know how to die. None of them have a quarrel with this thing, except us.'

I found the idea curious – animals having an opinion about death – so I cracked open another beer. 'Thinking about this isn't going to make a damned bit of difference,' I told him, but he wasn't listening. He was crying, soundlessly, tears pouring down his face.

'Whoah, boy, come on,' I said, putting my hand on his shoulder, but he stiffened up so I pulled my hand away. He was slumped opposite me, not making any attempt to hide his tears or wipe them away, crying not like a child, but the way a man cries, once or twice in his lifetime.

I had never thought he had those tears in him, and I didn't know why I didn't have those tears in me. He stopped eventually and shivered and said, with his teeth clenched, 'I always wanted, just once, to feel something, to feel everything, to feel existence until I couldn't stand it.' He looked over at me. 'Well now I do.'

I thought I understood him then, but I didn't know what to say. We sat there for a long time. Finally he said, 'I checked him every time I was here. His heart was fine.'

Frankly, I had never cared for those sessions with the stethoscope in Dad's study, the two of them listening to the deep thudding of his heart.

'It just gave out,' I said.

'Why?'

'Mother. That's why.'

'What are you talking about?'

'You haven't been here for six months,' I said, not wanting to blame him, just to make sure the facts were stated correctly. He banged his hand flat upon the table. 'Are you going to keep on saying, "You weren't here," for the rest of my life? He's dead. It's finished.'

I didn't mind him saying that. It didn't change what I thought, and at least he wasn't behaving as if what I said couldn't touch him. He was sounding like someone angry enough to want to hit me for not seeing things his way, and that was better than sounding like he couldn't be hurt.

'It's not finished. It's never going to be finished between us,' I said. I wasn't trying to provoke him, just making sure he knew where I stood.

He decided to ignore what I had just said. He took the envelope out of his trouser pocket again and spilled the contents out on to the table.

'Which do you want?'

'I'll take the throat lozenges,' I said.

'Get serious.'

'Put that stuff away.'

He wound my father's watch and held it in his hand for a moment and then he scooped the things back into the envelope and tossed me the half-pack of throat lozenges. I left them between us on the table.

'Well if you won't, I will,' and he shoved the envelope back into his pocket. 'Jack should have the watch, your wife should have the ring – and if you don't know that, you don't know a thing.' 'Jack and my wife are none of your goddamned business,' I said, and he fired back, 'He's my nephew,' and I said, 'Some uncle you are,' since I always had to remind him when Jack's birthday was. Yet instead of everything sliding out of control, like it seemed it might, it subsided and we sat there, across the kitchen table, with the lozenges and some crumpled empties between us.

'It was divide and rule,' I said eventually.

'That's just a cliché. It doesn't mean anything,' he said, looking into the bottom of his can of Coors. 'It wasn't him at all. It was between the two of us.'

'So what was it between us? Why have we got like this?' I wanted to know.

'There's no reason to put it down to him,' he said, matter-of-factly.

I got up and went over to the window. Beyond the porch light, I could see the mist hovering over the back field. It all came back so clearly I just began to speak. 'He's walking up the beach on the Jersey shore and the two of us are trailing behind him in the surf. First he gives you the stone he has picked up, and then you pass it to me, and then I throw it away. That's how it goes, right up the beach, until Mother disappears behind us in the glare. Then he turns back and we follow. That's how it always was. First he gives you the stone, then you give it to me, then I throw it away. What do you mean it had nothing to do with him? That was the whole story, right there.' I left him to think about that and went to the bathroom.

When I came back, he said, 'Forget it,' and I said, 'Sure.' We were both on our way to being drunk by then – which was a change, because I had never seen him drunk before, slumped over, all his nervous energy drained away. Whatever he said about not wanting to go back over it all, I could tell he was doing just that.

I didn't want to talk any more. It was obvious what had to be done, even though I still can't understand why I was so sure. I went over to the cupboard under the kitchen sink and found a pack of twenty black garbage bags. I left him in the kitchen and went up to my father's bedroom cupboard.

At least fifteen of my father's suits were hanging on the rail. Since he stopped working for the company, he had no reason to wear them, preferring a pair of old corduroys and a rollneck sweater, but he kept the suits in the closet. Once I found him standing there alone, just looking at them, as if contemplating the kind of man he had been when he wore them.

I knew where each had been purchased, what each looked like when he wore them, even why he had stopped wearing some of them and had banished them to the less used side of the rail. They were too small for me, and they were too small for my brother. My father had to accept that my brother had grown taller than he was, but you could tell he hated it really. 'What do you mean the thing doesn't fit you?' I remember him saying to my brother when he got him to try on one of his old suits. 'I'm telling you, look at the cuffs!' and I remember my father's face as he stared down at my brother's teenage ankles clearly showing beneath the cuffs. 'What the hell!' Father said. 'How d'you get so damn tall?' I remembered all this, so why did I need any of the suits?

None had a claim. None detained me: seersucker, worsted, tweed, pinstripe, cuffed, uncuffed, pleated, unpleated, Bloomingdales, Barneys, Harry Rosen, Stan Eley, Tip Top, the tuxedo with its skunk suspenders, which he wore to the company ball. None was spared. I was putting the last one in the bag, when my brother appeared in the doorway behind me.

'What do you think you're doing?'

'They don't fit you, and they don't fit me. So they're going to Goodwill in the morning.' I tossed him a black bag. 'Here, clear those drawers.'

It was the first time I had ordered him around, and I wasn't sure he would do what I told him, but I didn't care because I intended to keep on going, whether he helped me or not.

For a moment, he just stood there. Then he sat down on the bed and pulled open the chest of drawers in front of him. I watched him count twenty-six pairs of Father's socks, twenty-four sets of singlets and underwear, the drooping, shapeless variety he invariably wore. I was disposing of the shoes at the bottom of the suit cupboard, but I was seeing my father standing right beside us in the room, in his baggy underwear, reaching for his toes, failing, touching his knees, winking sideways in a pantomime of exercise, done only when his boys were watching; done, so he had said, for the sake of his heart.

My brother pushed Father's underwear into the black bag and rolled over on the bed, like a sick dog, his face buried in my father's pillows.

He whispered, 'Why can't you forget what you want to forget?'

I tuned the radio by the bed to a rock and roll station and went into the bathroom, opened the cabinet door above the sink and began emptying laxatives, hair tonic, bars of soap, four varieties of aspirin and painkillers into the black plastic bags. I counted ten pairs of tweezers in every shape and size and three different kinds of sleeping pills. My father, the hypochondriac.

Everything went into the bag, except Mother's sedation, the small green pills she took four times a day.

My brother was in the study by then and when I joined him he was spilling newspapers, letters, abstracts, review copies, reviews, files and clippings into the bags. I helped him out, and in twenty minutes we'd set loose an avalanche of paper which swept away our father's professional life.

In the white Olympia typewriter on his desk we found the first page of a speech to the Rotary Club in town, already dated for delivery on the following Friday night. Unlike my own speech, it would have been popular. He'd done it before, and farmers came in their pick-ups to hear my father giving his talk about soils and how to increase the yields. He had been in the middle of a sentence, but looking at it, I couldn't tell where it was headed. The rest of it was forming in his head, his hands were poised above the keys; those big hands with the purple twisting vein disappearing between the knuckles, like a river between mountains when seen from the sky. I could feel my memory of those hands begin to slip away, to lose definition, to become a memory of any hands, no longer his ones, which always smelled of hair tonic and soap.

She must have woken up from her nap and needed him for something. He had stopped, had walked her round the garden and then returned. He was going back to the typewriter. Then suddenly he felt tired, felt he should knock off for the day, so he had quit and gone downstairs and made himself a cup of coffee, and he had the paper in his hand and he was headed out to the garden chair by the rose bed, just fifteen feet across the gravel from the porch steps.

The half-sentence he had left behind in the typewriter began, 'As you all know, deep-disc ploughing will . . . ' Two rogue 'e's' floated above the word 'deep', like a disc plough itself, poised above a furrow. He had been saying he should get the key fixed. My brother leaned forward, ripped the page out of the machine and tore it up with his two hands.

In the top left-hand drawer of his desk, I found a thick bundle of business cards from soil scientists my father knew from around the world and several black Rexall notepads, filled with equations. The indentation of his pen was so vigorous and so deep you could feel it on the other side of the page.

In the top right-hand drawer, I found cheque books and a blizzard of unpaid bills: gas, electricity, water, credit cards. It was a surprise to see how chaotic it all was. From the bank statements, it was clear that he had just been going from one pension cheque to the next, hoping he could get by. I once offered to help him out, when he had said he was fed up with all the damned bills, and he had replied, 'Go away, boy. None of your business.'

'I'll handle these,' my brother said, but I didn't like that so I took the bills out of his hands and threw them into the garbage bag.

There was a fistful of photos in the bottom left-hand drawer and I fell into his chair to inspect them: there was one picture my mother had taken of the two of us, standing on either side of my father on the Jersey shore. We are all in bathing suits, and both our bodies look so white and slender and weak compared to his. We are both shading our eyes from the sun, and I am leaning against my father's side with my arm round his waist. My brother holds himself an inch or so away from Father and is standing straighter than I am. Father has a knotted handkerchief on his head, which my mother always said made him look peculiar, since he was the only man on the Jersey shore to wear one like that. 'But I *am* peculiar!' my father roars. 'It is why you married me, woman.' It was one of his better moments.

I didn't care about photographs. Everything was in my mind, and I wanted to keep it that way. My brother was carrying round a brown envelope of his keepers – small items like the photograph, Nettie's silk fragment, Dad's Parker pen – but I didn't want a thing.

There was one photograph in the drawer which neither

of us could identify. Yellowed with age, it showed a man in a tight collar and a suit with all three buttons done up, standing in a garden. You couldn't tell anything about him from the way he stared back at you, the hint of a smile on his lips, his eyes squinting into the sun, in the middle of an unidentified garden with a pine tree behind him in soft focus. Beside him stood a woman in a cloche hat and a smart three-quarter length dress. There was something about the curve of her lips and the resentful look in her eyes that made you feel she was capable of dealing in malice and hurt. They both had their hands on the shoulders of a boy in short pants and slicked down hair. The boy might have been my father's twin brother, who had died in Constantinople, and it might have been my father, but then if it was, he probably would have shown us the picture and he never had. My brother turned the photograph over. On the back it was stamped, 'Abdullah Freres, Constantinople'. My brother put it in his shirt pocket.

Once I asked my father about Odessa. He told me what I wanted to know and what his father did and how he got to Paris and then to the States at the beginning of the Depression. When I asked him why he talked about it so little, he said, 'You know why? So people wouldn't ask me fool questions.' I said I just wanted to know, and couldn't see why he wouldn't tell me more, and he said, 'there's nothing back there. Nothing. Believe me.'

Perhaps that was why he never talked about Odessa, why he let it go. Not just so that he would be free of it. But so that his sons would be free too, whether they wanted to be or not.

That photograph was the last thing to detain us. After that, my brother turned up the radio, and all the staplers, loose change, paperclips, erasers, stubby pencils tumbled into the bags, along with address books, all their friends' names and telephone numbers, the whole network of their life, in an advanced state of disintegration, held together by elastic bands. Who were those people to me now?

My brother picked up my father's desk diary and flipped through it. 'Look,' he said, 'a doctor's appointment at the medical centre tomorrow afternoon. So he knew something was wrong.' As if the futility of being a doctor and not even being able to save your own father had finally become too much for him, he whirled round and hurled the diary at the wall. The spine split and pages flew through the air and scattered all over the floor. I left him leaning against the wall with his eyes shut.

Downstairs in the kitchen, I threw away three cupboards full of groceries, rotting fruit in bowls, wilted flowers in vases. In the basement I dragged up suitcases, hair dryers, tennis rackets, jump cables, pairs of skates, shirts hanging up by the washing machine, and old shoes marked with the stain of his feet and the shape of his toes in the insoles. His feet were so small for such a big man.

If I could have, I would have ripped the pictures off the hooks, the hooks out of the walls, the carpets off the floors, the covers off the sofas. I could have torched the place. As if to say: you took him, so take the rest, so take everything. As if to say, I don't want to remember anything, this appointment book, this suit still holding his shape, this photograph of him squinting into the sun, this scarf filled with the warm smell of his neck. I wanted to forget everything. I wanted to lose it all. I felt flames roaring in my head and my heart was full of savage joy.

Then twenty black garbage bags were full and it was a new day. I dragged them out to the car and loaded them in, half to go to Goodwill and half to the dump. The flowers in the beds looked limp so I turned on the sprinkler and went up on the porch and sat down to watch the water spin. Then it occurred to me that it didn't matter if the flowerbeds were watered or not.

My brother came out and handed me a beer and we sat together, with our feet stretched out in the sun, watching the water sprinkler pointlessly watering the flowers. I rolled the beer can across my cheek and considered what we had done. I felt clear in my mind. This house, I believed, had been inhabited by illness and I had purified it. This place had been possessed. I had cleansed it.

My brother did not say anything, but I followed the direction of his eyes from the porch steps to the retaining wall, fifteen feet away. Amongst the footprints and the tyre-tracks of the ambulance, you could still make out the deep, ragged furrows left behind by my father's knees when he had dragged his body to the retaining wall.

ON OUR WAY down to the city in my car, I said, 'We should have told him, "Dad, enough is enough." Why didn't we take over? What was the matter with us?' It was as if I had seen it all coming, not for a millisecond, but for a year, and had stood there, speechless, unable to move, to warn, to avert what was sure to happen: my father's heart just giving out, leaving her, as he believed she would be, defenceless in the world. Looking out at the highway and the cars we were passing, my brother said, 'We didn't have it in us. We were just a pair of sons, and he was our father and that was all there was to it.'

Glancing over at him in the passenger seat, I realised that I was the only person in the world who knew exactly why this man had to look this way and no other, why he had the muscular full-faced look of a family of Scottish farmers and preachers and the deep-set eyes – 'It's the Mongols, boy,' my father used to say – that had run in a grain merchant's family from Odessa.

'We're sons. What can I say?' he repeated.

Now, we both knew, we had to become parents.

He thought for a while, and the airport ramp came up, and he said 'We sell it?'

I nodded. At the departures ramp, he took the envelope out of his pocket, and stuffed the watch and the ring into my shirt pocket. I was going to say something, but he shook his head, to make any further refusal impossible, and then he was gone, striding through the glass doors, his face, no longer a brother's, no longer a son who has just buried a father, but a face suddenly unknown to me again, the mask of a professional man hurrying to make a flight.

A friend told me the thing to look for in a nursing home was laundry trolleys. 'Forget the hardsell about compassion and concern,' she said. 'Just look for laundry trolleys.' I saw a lot of stinking laundry trolleys, a lot of corridors lined with wheelchairs, and people strapped into them, their old, mussed heads lolling forwards onto plastic bibs smeared with food. The smell of urine followed me out into the street. I sat in the car and smoked and thought about my father and what he would think if he knew what I was doing. I had made promises to him and I wanted to keep them, but there could be a time when it just isn't possible, when there isn't enough money left and you have to choose between sacrificing yourself and sacrificing somebody else. I told myself that if I didn't get my mother into a secure environment with twenty-four hour care, I would spend the rest of my life worrying about what might happen. I couldn't tell whether my mother still had it in her to escape, but I wasn't about to take any more chances. My mother was in her sixties. I knew she might live for a long time with this condition, and that if I cared for her myself, I would have to give my whole life away. I told myself this, over and over, but it didn't make any difference.

So I stubbed out my cigarette and started up the car and set off to my last call. It was an eighty-bed private facility in the centre of town, a bus ride away from our house, so I could visit her as often as I wanted, with a single room available which we could afford, for however long it took, provided we sold the farm. If there had been decent public health insurance, we wouldn't have had to sell, but there wasn't, because this is the land of the free and the home of the brave, and Father's private plans weren't up to the cost. At that moment, I had no feelings about selling the house at all. Indeed, I couldn't bear the thought of setting my feet inside it again.

When it came time to putting my mother in the institution, my brother said he would come up. I said he needn't bother, and he laughed and said we had better share out the guilt. So that was how we did it. We shared out the guilt, with me carrying Mother's suitcase, and my brother holding her hand and carrying a painting of the farm that we were allowed to put up in front of her bed. In the lobby, there were some old people in wheelchairs with bibs round their chins watching television. One had her arm in a sling, another old man had his head shaved and stitches from the base of his neck to above his ear. You could see the white nylon tips of the stitches poking through the black congealed blood along the scar line. Mother looked at this and looked at us, and we didn't know what to say.

When we came out of the elevator on to her floor, a small man who looked Italian tried to take my hand, and an old woman in a wheelchair, with huge black eyes, began cooing and beckoning. Next to her in the hallway was a Chinese woman who was asleep, strapped to a chair and beside her a huge black man, between forty and fifty years old, with muscular arms, who was tied to a chair, so he wouldn't fall out. He was raising and lowering his head, over and over, and his eyes were shut. I hurried Mother past all of this, as if I thought I could spare her seeing any of it.

Her room was in the corner, next to the shower room, and through the closed door we could hear the water going and someone calling out, in a cracked voice, 'Mary! Mary! Mary!' Over the sound of the shower, a nurse shouted, 'Mary isn't here,' but it didn't make any difference, for the cries continued. We tried not to listen and concentrated instead on the L-shaped room, painted bright yellow, with a linoleum floor which reflected our blurred shapes and a view over the flat roof of the church next door. In the centre was a hospital bed with a metal frame to hold the patient in and a call button laying on the pillow. My brother began unpacking her suitcase and putting her things in the chest of drawers, but I took over and so he sat down on the bed beside my mother, him in his blue suit, she in her turquoise drip-dry nylon dress, side by side, not touching. My mother stared out of the window, absently smoothing the coverlet of the bed with her right hand. I sat down beside her, took her hand in mine and gently slid her wedding ring from her finger. It was one of the regulations in this place. Some patients cut themselves with their rings. Some patients swallowed them. She let me take her ring away, not once taking her gaze off the traffic streaming up the avenue. Then I stood up and said 'Bye, Mother. We'll be back later.'

'No,' she suddenly said, not looking at us. 'No, no, no.'

'Mother,' I began.

'Don't say that. I'm not having it,' and then with such feeling that we both went quite still: 'I can't stand it. I can't.'

'What, Mother? Tell me.' I was down on my knees in front of her. She looked at me straight in the eyes – cornered, enraged, helpless.

Then she said, 'Go away.'

'Mother.'

'Get out.'

When I visited her a week later, she wasn't in her room and she wasn't in the hall. 'Try the TV room,' they said at the nursing station. Six patients were dozing in front of a TV set fixed high on the wall. An old East Indian man in a tracksuit and pair of slippers was asleep on his wife's shoulder. She was wearing a sari and was reading a newspaper in her own language. A big black man was strapped into his wheelchair next to her and was grinding his teeth while watching a woman on TV demonstrating bleach powder in front of a washing machine. The colour balance was so bad that the woman on the television had an orange shimmer all around her body, as if she was radioactive, but nobody seemed to notice. The old Chinese woman was turned to the wall, making spitting noises. Two old ladies were sitting side by side, ignoring the TV and gazing out at the traffic. One of them was tiny, like a sparrow, with a sparrow's black eyes and the same tiny, darting movements. Next to her in the corner was another old woman in a pink Terylene dress, sunk in her chair, staring out of the window.

'Hello, Mother,' I said.

'Hello,' she said, as if she had never been anywhere else.

I took her arm, and we walked down the corridor, past the nursing room, where the supervisor looked up and said, 'Hi, hon,' as she went by. We passed the rooms with old people lying asleep with their mouths open and reached the alarmed fire-escape door at the end of the hall and the picture window which overlooked some garages and back gardens. She looked down at the barbecues, at an empty children's swing between two trees and a Pontiac with its trunk tied down with rope.

'How is it here, Mother?'

'How is it where?'

'Here, where you are.'

She said nothing, just looked down at the life she had left – the swing – the barbecue and the car, as if they were remains of a lost civilisation.

In the long shiny corridor, the air-conditioning hummed. A wheelchair squeaked on the linoleum. The small Italian man, known as the Barber, peeked his head around the door of his room and then shuffled back inside. Pills rattled in a bottle; someone sighed in another room. At the elevators, I stood and waited, feeling the inert, drugged lifelessness of the place seeping into me. When the elevator doors opened, I got in and did not look back. I looked at my watch. My visit had lasted seven minutes.

I couldn't tell the least thing about my mother's state of mind. The illness still allowed her a small margin of manoeuvre. She could still have thoughts about her thoughts. She could still ask herself what she thought of being in this place, and as far as I could see she no longer cared where she was or thought about the life she had left behind. I couldn't bear this. The next time I visited, I asked her whether she remembered the brush fire in the back field, when I was sixteen.

She was down to simple sentences – subject, verb, predicate – which seemed to compress everything to essentials. 'Yes, Dad put it out.'

Father's name bobbed up into the stream of her speech like a stick or a piece of grass and then floated away. I don't think she ever mentioned him again.

I see Father in his bathing trunks and high boots, his body smeared with soot and sweat, rushing to and fro with the hose spraying down the grass ahead of the fire. The ragged line of flame, whipped by an August wind, is a hundred yards from the house and he is shouting at me over his shoulder, 'We're losing it! Get the car out of the garage!'

I am in the front seat of our Dodge, with the trunk full of tins and the lawn mower and the jerry cans of fuel, trying to get the thing to start. Please start for me. Come on. It won't turn over. Oh God, please.

Mother is with him out in the field, tamping down the smouldering patches with a shovel, but you would never know that, looking at her now, in the chair by the window in her room, looking vaguely at my distressed face.

I want to relive the scene with her. I want to say, 'Don't you remember how the wind shifted, how it carried the fire right down to the pond and doused it there, and how Father came back to the garage, and even though the danger was over, he yanked me out of the car, took my place and started it up first time, backed it past me down the driveway so fast the tyres were spitting gravel, turned off the ignition and then went back into the house to have a shower, glaring at me for being the useless, panicky disappointment that I was to him.' I wanted to say, 'And how you watched and didn't stand up for me for trying?'

But I didn't say anything. I looked at her bleak, expressionless face and thought about all the days, weeks, months, years, bearing us two boys, making love to him, being in tears, being full of hatred towards him, anything, and all of it vanished as if it had never happened. She just seemed relieved to be done with the whole thing. She was pleased to see me, in a faint sort of a way, but I don't believe I was in her thoughts when I was gone. On the walls of the stark yellow room where she spent most of the day, there was only one painting – the farmhouse and the orchard in bright sunshine – which might make her remember. There were no Chinese dishes in the sink to make her wonder: shouldn't I be washing these? There was no one whose name she had to struggle to recall, nobody who seemed to think something was wrong. There was the shining linoleum corridor; there was the bed with the steel bars on the side; there was the window looking over the roof of the Korean Baptist Church. There was me. That was all.

She would let me hold her hand and take her out for a walk in the park opposite and buy her an ice-cream, always chocolate, always eaten on the same bench, always enjoyed with the same words, 'This is the best I've had.' Then she would hand me the empty cup and the plastic spoon and I would throw it away for her, and we would walk back to the home, and I would say, 'Goodbye, Mother,' at the lift, and I would watch the steel doors close upon her.

Perhaps she was grieving for him too, in her bleached and faded way, just staring out of the window, watching the traffic streaming past. Maybe that is what her mourning came down to, staring, waiting for the time to pass, for the feeling to go away.

The brush fire is out. I am standing in the yard, in the acrid air, and I can hear my father's singing in the shower reaching me through the open bathroom window. Mother is watching me from the kitchen, saying nothing. I am thinking, Why does this have to go on? When will I ever escape?

He always had an unbelievable capacity to forget what he wanted to forget, so that now he comes downstairs, dressed only in a towel, with his hair still wet from the shower, and strides past me out into the field to check on the fire, as if nothing has happened, as if he hasn't left me standing there, wishing the ground would swallow me up.

That day, I did want him to die. Now he was dead and I could scarcely stand up for the sorrow inside me.

*

I took a couple of weeks' leave after putting Mother in the home and then I went back to class. I don't know how I got through that year, because there were a lot of moments, standing there with my notes on the lectern, when I wouldn't really know how I was going to get to the end of the hour. A hole would open up in time and I would disappear into it. I wouldn't be thinking of him exactly, but of some inconsequential memory, like the swish of the lawn sprinkler outside my bedroom window at night and the indistinct murmur of my parents' voices, talking quietly so they wouldn't wake us, while they sat up drinking together by the light of the porch lamp. It was as if mourning allowed me to return to such moments but not to return to my feelings.

Then I would come to and all those faces in class would be staring at me, wondering what was going on. I can't remember anything I taught them for the rest of that year. Looking back, I think this was the moment when I began to uncouple from my job. It seemed to make so little difference. Whatever thoughts, whatever propositions entered my head, they were powerless to bring sensation back to the numb regions inside me. Nothing I read remained with me. Nothing I said seemed important. At one departmental meeting I went to, one of my colleagues, a woman who taught the other section of the introductory course, actually waved her hand in front of my face in the middle of a meeting, to see whether I was still there. I wasn't.

I had a feeling of shame about my grief, as if I was making false amends for the bitterness I had felt towards him when he was alive. I wanted to remember him as we were together and not to forget that our quarrels had been necessary, but as time went on, I couldn't bear to remember my anger and his.

I admit I must have been impossible to live with. It was the self-righteousness of the grieving – my idea that I would betray him if I carried on as before, if I went through the motions of living – that must have driven my family apart from me. I still do not understand those instincts that lead you to flee the ones who want to help you, that lead you to take revenge upon them for a sorrow that is not their fault. I look back over this period and scarcely understand anything I did. I felt in the grip of some fatality, when in fact I could have stopped myself at any moment. After a life of apparent sanity and self-control, I discovered reservoirs of gratuitous destructiveness I had never imagined I possessed. Looking back now, I seem to have been entranced by it, enraptured by my capacity to do harm.

After about three months, my wife began to get impatient with me, with the fact that all I wanted to do was watch television or go to the nursing home, with the fact that I felt cut off from everyone, including her and the children. I could see this was how she felt, but it made me angry that she didn't let me go through everything in my own time.

'But I am letting you go through it. It's all I can do.'

It was after dinner one night in our kitchen, and I was seeking my own hurt and hers.

'You're bored with the whole thing, aren't you?' I said.

'Don't start.'

'You are. You think, "I've got kids here and a house to run, and he can't snap out of it. All he does is go down to that damned nursing home and sit and talk to his mother, who can't talk about anything anyway." That's what you think.'

'Why are you doing this?' she said to me, throwing the dishtowel across the kitchen counter, where it knocked over the radio. 'I know what you're going through.'

'But it bores you,' I said, circling around the edge of the kitchen, because I was sure I was right about this.

'No, it doesn't bore me. I just think you're going to have to . . . '

'Pull myself together.'

'Don't put words into my mouth.'

'That's what you're thinking.'

She lit a cigarette and blew the smoke out. 'All right, that is what I think.'

I wanted to take this as far as it would go. I wanted to get it all out, so I said,

'Because I've never grown up. Because I'm forty-five years old, and I'm still tied hand and foot to the pair of them.' She let me say it all. She didn't stop me.

'Even though one of them is dead, and the other one might as well be. Isn't that what you think?'

'You're doing fine all by yourself,' she said.

I slammed my hand down on the table and I got up very close to her so that she was forced to look me in the face and I said, very quietly, 'I have to go through this. I have to keep the faith that I have. And you better understand.'

Then her eyes darted away and I turned and saw Jack watching both of us from the kitchen door.

'Goddammit, Jack,' she said. 'Give us a moment to work something out, will you?'

'No,' I said, 'You stay right where you are.' I shouldn't have done this, but I couldn't stop. 'You've got the right to hear everything between us. You're old enough. So here it is, Your mother thinks I shouldn't be carrying on about my dad, shouldn't be carrying on about my mother. That I should just grow up and act my age.

That's what she thinks, isn't it? Why don't you just say it to your own son, instead of walking around feeling superior?'

I could see all the grey in my wife's hair, all the wear in her face and all the hurt I caused, but I couldn't stop the bitterness from pouring out of me. She was looking at me as if she didn't know who I was, as if our twenty-one years together were nothing. Jack's face was white and still. He wanted to get out of there, but I had told him to stay. I needed to implicate him, to draw him in and force him to take my side against her. Even then I knew I shouldn't have, but nothing was going to stop me.

'Because you always felt superior. Ever since I can remember, you've been thinking, "Why the hell doesn't he stand up to them? Why does he let them walk all over him? Why does he clean up after every goddamned one of them?" '

'Jack,' my wife said, 'you go to your room, right now.'

Jack looked at me, and I said nothing. He waited there for a moment and then he ran upstairs and slammed the door to his bedroom.

My wife and I stood there, across the kitchen table, our heads down, our hands gripping the tops of the kitchen chairs. Even then, some part of me that wasn't insane with rage was also thinking, 'Look at that, even our gestures, even the way we grip these chairs, are the same.'

Finally she said, 'You know something? I didn't believe all those things until you said them, but now that you've said them, I do.'

There were tears in her eyes when she said, 'I really do not understand.' She turned away and stood by the sink, with her hands braced on the counter. I could have stopped it right there. I could have come up and put my hands on her shoulders and said I was sorry. I even saw myself doing it, but I knew she would shake me off, knew she would stiffen, knew she would refuse me, so I didn't. I turned and went out the door.

Although it was after dark, I jumped into the car and went over to the nursing home and sat up with my mother till the nurses came and said it was time for me to go home.

That might have been the end of it. We had fought about these things before. I knew I couldn't change what she thought, but that hadn't stopped us working ourselves back to some kind of accommodation. This time it was different. I still think that if my mother and father had been there, we might have pulled it back in time. You might think that was just what my wife said was wrong with me, that everything depended on my parents' being there. But it was true. I would never have said those things to her that night and ruined everything, had they not been true. It was obvious to me, even then, that my father might have knocked some sense into my head. My mother might have walked me out into the orchard, heard me out and then told me to go back home to my wife and apologise. But they weren't there. I did try to talk to my brother on the phone. I said, 'I can't seem to stop. Ever since he died, I've been throwing everything away and I can't seem to stop.'

'And you think I can help you with that?' he replied. I said I had no time for the impersonal scientist routine and hung up on him. Now I understand it differently. He meant that once you begin throwing your life away, you have to go through it until the compulsion to destroy has run its course. He never told me how he knew this.

It was another of those things about him I had to take on trust.

MIRANDA WAS A quiet woman, petite and dark, with a small gold cross round her neck. She came from Mindanao in the Philippines and she spoke with a soft Asian accent. It always perplexed me that some nurses seemed possessed of an intuitive natural tenderness towards their patients while others did not. When you watched them pulling a shirt off the withered shoulders of some old man in the shower room, you could see that they knew how to do it gently, and that you didn't need to tell them what dignity was, because they showed they knew what it was in every one of their gestures. There were others, not necessarily less decent people, who had to have procedures to behave decently, who had no natural intuition for what would insult the honour of strangers. It was as if some knew how to feel the pain of their patients without being frightened of it, while others felt they had to keep it at a proper professional distance. I got so that I could tell the moment a nurse approached my mother, whether they had this secret capacity or whether it was just a job for them. Miranda was one of those who had the gift, and it has to be called a gift because it is something in human beings that cannot be taught. You could see how she lifted my mother from a chair, how she exactly judged the guiding pressure of her arm so that my mother would not feel she was being pulled or led, but was choosing the way on her own.

My mother seemed to sense the tacit understanding that flowed through Miranda's touch. Other nurses were struck; other nurses were screamed at, when some line, invisible to anyone but the most sensitive, was crossed. Miranda seemed to know where that line lay. She seemed to hear the messages my mother tapped out through the walls of her prison.

Miranda said to me, 'Your mother is a special person.'

'Why do you say that?'

'She is intelligent, understands more than the others. Like if I say, time for your bath, she says, "We must do as we are told," like she knows that it is not supposed to be like this, she should be bathing herself. And like another time, when you had gone, I say: "Your son is good to you," and your mother thought about that and she says, "Funny boy," as if she tried to understand you, was still trying, you know?'

Miranda nodded as she filled out the evening prescription sheet behind the nursing station. 'They tell us many things.' I liked the way Miranda talked about my mother and I said so.

'You look sad. Father dies. I read the case notes, sorry.'

'That's all right.'

'You want to hold on to her as long as you can.'

'Yes, I do.'

'You want her to help you.'

'Why do you say that?'

'I can see.'

I felt like going down the hall to take a look at myself in the mirror. Why was I giving myself away like this? But I put it down to Miranda's gift. If she could see that I wanted my mother to help me, it had to be true.

'It is always like this at the beginning. I see them. Sons

and daughters, they visit a lot from the beginning, like they hope for something.'

'What for?'

She stopped writing and looked up at me, shyly. 'I don't know. At the beginning, these people visit every day. Sitting beside their mother, their father, all day sometime, waiting for them to say something.'

'Say something,' I laugh. 'Anything.'

She nodded and looked down at a prescription sheet, ticking off the dosages she had just administered.

'Then they give up, right?'

'Then,' she said, still writing, 'they leave them to us.'

'I'm not going to leave her to you,' I said.

'Maybe,' she said, and I took this, not as a challenge or as a judgement, but as a warning, as if she wondered whether I realised what the future had in store. She had worked on this ward for years and knew what was ahead for me. I envied what she knew and wondered whether she would ever tell me.

'I'm going to stay,' I said, trying to sound different from all the others whom Miranda had seen walking away from their parents, never to return.

Miranda knew that my mother rarely spoke and looked away when I kissed her, and never gave me proof that she cared whether I came or not.

'Not because I have to,' I said. 'Because I need to.' This seemed to embarrass her, because she got up and put the prescription folder into the file and turned her back to me. I was embarrassed myself, and wondered what it was about her that made me so confessional, that made me tell her that being with my mother had become the only part of my life I fully respected.

'I understand,' said Miranda, turning to look at me.

*

After a couple of months, I began walking Miranda home after her shifts, because her apartment was on the way to my bus stop. Eventually, one evening, she asked me to come up. When we got inside the door of her apartment, she stood on tiptoes, touched my face with her hands and kissed me.

I wasn't used to being with someone who knew so little about me, who didn't know all the things that had gone wrong. I was so unused to being with someone who took me as I was, that I didn't feel I should be there. But she knew what she wanted and I didn't and so I let it happen.

Lying there in her basement studio apartment, looking up at a poster of Manila Bay on her wall, and smelling this woman beside me asleep, strange to me, different in every detail from the one woman I was used to and knew all the way through to her very bones, I began crying.

What was it? Release from the vice of grieving and coping and being a husband and not knowing, day to day, how I could keep going at my job? And shame, too. I couldn't understand why a man so frightened of intimacy should be spending a night with a woman who was unlike anyone he had ever been with before. Even now, I don't know whether to be glad or distressed that it happened. I do think I may be the sort of man who should never let desire get in the way of his need to be understood. For that was what Miranda had in such mysterious abundance, the gift of silent, attentive, watchful understanding. Why was I not content with that? Why more? Why this naked body beside me so unprotected and trusting, her arm lying across my chest?

After a while, those feelings ebbed away too, and I just lay there, naked, cold, feeling how ridiculous it was that a grown man, with children and a job and responsibilities, should lose his parents and be unable to do anything about it but lie beside a strange woman and weep.

*

Had I wanted to, there were plenty of ways to keep my wife from finding out. I could have decided that it didn't matter. I could have kept a secret. But I was in the grip of some fatal confusion between truthfulness and destructiveness, so I told her everything, three weeks later, in a monotone I barely recognised as my own.

She said, 'I want you out of here in an hour.'

I said I wanted to be the one who explained to the children, but she looked at me and shook her head. I thought, as I packed my bag, furiously throwing my clothes in, that one day they would hear my version.

You can betray your family and walk out into the night feeling you have done the only honourable thing. That was how it was. I was out of there in less than an hour, with one suitcase, leaving my children behind, upstairs in their beds, and my wife with her back turned to me, smoking cigarette after cigarette, letting the ash drop into the kitchen sink with a hiss.

I moved into a furnished studio on the sixth floor of a sixties block across the park from the nursing home, with a pull-out sofa bed, a dirty sliding window giving out over the park, a refrigerator that hummed so loud I had to unplug it, and some stains on the carpet that made it seem as if the previous tenant had bled to death. But I was so far gone that I didn't care. It was twenty minutes from Miranda's place and it was a minute's walk from the nursing home. From my window, I could see across the park above the trees to the window of my mother's room.

There is almost nothing a person will not do in order to be understood. They will even pull their life apart so that what was not understood can at last be seen, like a wound. That was how I felt.

I took the fact that my wife couldn't understand why I had to be with my mother, had to see her every day, had to attend to every single thing she needed, as if this was the proof that my wife had never grasped who I really was.

I also believed that there was some primary attachment in me that my wife could never, had never, accepted. Since my father's death, I had been mourning something larger than one life. It had been our whole existence at the farm, that whole world of mine now destroyed by illness. Why my wife couldn't let me mourn that, I didn't understand. If she wouldn't, I had no choice but to do it somewhere else.

I stood there, the first night, and I thought about the farm and the path I had taken to this dirty apartment. I thought of my life like a gravity wall – one of those fine stone walls that marked the western property line of the farm. Those walls had been built by the first farmers to clear the land. They had pulled the stones out of the fields and had stacked them along the lines of their farms in the days when the fields were full of stumps and the crops were thin and ragged. The stone walls had survived the passing of the men who had built them and the farms they had raised. They would hold for ever against the wind and the ice, but if you happened to remove one or two stones on purpose, a whole section of it would just collapse. That was what had happened to my life. I had pulled the wall down with my own hands. The one light there was seemed to come from my mother's bedroom window.

Once in the autumn I took my children up to the farm to help me finish cleaning up before we put it on the market. The grass was wet and waist-high in the fields, and there were weeds poking up through the gravel. Inside, the house was cold and damp. Dead insects lay on the floors by the windows, cobwebs caught your face in the dark, and all the objects – the chairs, the tables, the sofa – had the subdued, suffering air of people in a funeral home, gathered to view a coffin. I told the children they could take away something to remember the place by. Jack didn't want to touch anything.

'Why not?'

'I just don't.'

'Come on, Jack, tell me.'

He held me responsible for everything. And he didn't want to take anything from me. I said, 'Look, none of this stuff is mine. It's your grandad's and grandmother's and they would want you to have something.' He still wouldn't, and he went out into the back pasture and walked to the top of the hill and sat there, staring down at me, while Sally followed me round as I cleaned out the place and filled up the trunk of the car. Sally didn't mind being helpful, but I could see her wondering to herself whether I was still someone she could trust.

I was carrying the TV across the gravel to put it in the back of the car, when she said, 'Why do we have to do this?' I put the TV down in the trunk and walked inside with her and sat down at the kitchen table. 'Something came to an end here,' I said. 'I wish it hadn't, but it did and now we have to sell it and go on to the next thing if we can.' She listened to this but she still didn't see why; and, to tell the truth, neither did I.

I went into the garage and got up on the stepladder and pulled the weapon off its hooks and found the pack of ammunition among the screws and the nails and headed up to the pasture. I loaded it while walking, and when I got up to where Jack was, on the top of the hill, I handed it to him. He looked up and said, 'She hates guns, you know that.'

'I know what your mother thinks, but I want you to have this. It was mine, and now it's yours.'

Jack was hunched up, with his arms wrapped round his knees, looking down at the house.

'What am I going to do with a gun in the city?' he said.

I wasn't going to beg my own son and I wasn't going to pretend I wasn't hurt either, so I whirled round and quick fired some rounds into the trees. It made Jack jump. Then I walked back down to the garage and replaced the weapon on the hooks.

I went back into the house and closed up. The car was full and I had taken out everything I had room for, particularly her portrait of me and the painting of the Antigonish headland. My wife was prepared to let me store some boxes in the basement, and the rest I was going to send to my brother or sell. I didn't have any room in my studio apartment. I went from room to room, turning off the heating and the lights, and then just stood there for a while listening to the house settling and cooling and the cracking of the radiators going cold.

As my daughter came down the porch steps behind me, I could hear a faint jingling sound. I turned round and there in her hand was the bowl holding the remaining beads of my mother's necklace.

On the drive back to the city, she fell asleep with the bowl in her lap and when I dropped my children off at my wife's, I carried her up the front steps, passed her to my wife and handed her the bowl of beads. She took them without a word.

WHENEVER THE PHONE went that winter, I either knew who it was before I picked it up or I didn't answer. If it was Thursday night, it was Miranda, just coming off shift. If it was Sunday morning, it was my brother, just back from his run, checking in on me and Mother. The rest of the time, it hardly rang at all. I managed to hold down my job, but nobody from the college got in touch. A hard time tends to create an irradiated zone around you, and so most evenings, when I got back from the nursing home, the phone never went. It did ring late one Wednesday evening in the middle of February, just three rings, before it went dead. I knew who it was. I walked around the place for about half an hour wondering whether I should call her back. The longing didn't go away, and half of the time I did not know why I didn't give in to it.

One day the following spring, I was in a supermarket near our old house and I saw her at the end of an aisle; she had her hair done in a new way, up off her face, and she looked like someone who had never known me and had never needed me. I sneaked out of the supermarket and went back to the nursing home and sat there for an hour with my mother, not saying anything, but wondering how a man who wanted to marry like his parents had married, who wanted to stay true the way they had stayed true, had got himself so lost so that his own wife was a stranger to him.

When I left her, I must have assumed that she would stay

as she was, rooted to the spot, waiting for me to return. I never imagined that she wouldn't wait, that she would go out and begin living the life that I had denied her. And now she was.

I got up every morning, went to school, got through the day, came by the nursing home at about six and would help Mother have her dinner. It was a good time to be with her, four of them to a table, feeding Mother with a spoon when she couldn't manage, most of the time just watching her labour to feed herself with fork and knife, watching her relapse, give up and stare into space, until I took the fork and knife from her hand. After that I would go back to the apartment and heat up something out of a tin. Miranda got Friday night off, so I usually spent it at her place, eating take-out and watching television. Looking back, it was not much of an existence, but it had a point to it. Miranda's way of explaining what I was doing was to say that I needed time. For what? I wondered. Would I still be with her at the end of that time? I couldn't say. I had never lived like this before. All my life – I had married at twenty-four – I had lived within the lines of a discernible future, my children growing up, my work, my wife and I growing together, my parents growing older. Suddenly, I couldn't tell what was going to happen next. Some nights with Miranda, I felt nothing but exhilaration; some nights, I wondered how I was going to get through the next five minutes. I couldn't understand what I was doing with this woman who said so little, who sat beside me on the couch, watching television, stroking my neck, as if there was some knot there she thought her hands could smooth away. As always, she conveyed the impression that she understood me, and that was what kept me where I was, depending on her silent intuition for pain.

*

We got an offer on the farm in the spring. It was close enough to what we were asking, so I phoned my brother and told him he should come up and help me to close the deal.

When I picked him up at the airport and said the three of us should go straight to the house, my brother walked me away from Miranda down to a corner of the parking lot. He said he wasn't sure it was such a good idea for Miranda to come along. 'Family business,' he said, looking down at his feet, embarrassed and also angry that I didn't seem to understand.

I said it just wasn't negotiable. 'She got me through the winter.' He looked at me and shook his head and we rejoined Miranda at the car.

The three of us drove up from the airport and when we got out, I opened the house for my brother and left him to go through the rooms, choosing what he wanted, while I stayed outside, sitting on the low wall. The flowerbeds were all overgrown, and there was grass in the gravel, and I was just thinking I should get down and weed the place, when the buyers rolled up in their Mercedes.

They were a childless couple in their early forties. He was a partner in a law firm and she was something in antiques and they were going to turn it into their country place. I didn't want to hear where they were going to put the swimming pool or how they were going to redecorate the interior, so I just took out the documents and told them my lawyer had gone through them and my brother was inside taking a final look and then we could all sign and get it over with. I held Miranda's hand when I said this, and I was glad she was there, she being what there was to my new life.

When my brother came out onto the porch, he had

Mother's painting of the three figures under his arm. The buyer and his wife made a fuss of him, because they had seen him on a television programme, explaining brain function, but he didn't have any time for that.

'Let's get down to business,' he said and so we spread the deeds of sale out on the front porch, in the thin April sunlight, and with Miranda as our witness, the two of us signed the place away. 'You'll find some things here,' I said as I handed them the keys, thinking of the rifle on the hook in the garage, 'and you're welcome to them.' The buyers wanted us to come in and have a drink, but my brother shook his head.

Neither of us looked back as we drove away and not a word passed between us all the way into the city. Miranda sat up front between the two of us, and I covered her hand with mine and drove with the other, while my brother just stared out of the window at the other farms and all the pieces of property on either side of the road that meant something to people.

I drew up outside the nursing home, turned off the ignition and we sat there for a moment. It was my brother who snapped out of it first. Miranda was watching him, and he said, 'I don't blame you for not understanding, I really don't,' and she looked embarrassed because she hadn't said anything.

Neither of us could understand what we had done, though there were any number of good reasons for it. The money was needed to keep Mother in the home. I had two establishments to support, and my brother, who could have made a fortune as a clinician, had gone into research. And then there were the other reasons. The life we had lived at the farm was over. My marriage was over. The reasons for selling were evident, but at that moment, sitting in my car in front of the nursing home, none of them felt convincing.

'I know what,' my brother said, jumping out of the car, 'Let's give her a surprise.' He didn't say what it was, but he went upstairs to get her ready, and I remained in the car, wondering why he was so cheerful.

'Your brother is a strange man,' Miranda said while we were waiting.

'Feel strange myself,' I said.

She covered my hand on the steering wheel with her hand. But she was still thinking of him.

'He is too hard.' I shook my head. 'Hard, no. He just doesn't mess up people the way I seem to do. I wish I were harder.'

As we settled my mother into the car, my brother suddenly said, out of nowhere, 'Who remembers *The Court Jester*? Come on, how does it go?'

There we were in the Alton Broadview, Father pounding our knees, rather than his own, when it came to a funny part, and my mother laughing so hard she began whispering, 'Stop, stop, stop.' Danny Kaye was my father's favourite actor and he always said he would have married Glynis Johns, who co-starred in the picture, had he not been otherwise engaged. 'It's her voice, you understand,' he said, to which my mother replied with a laugh, 'the hell it is,' thinking of how Glynis Johns looked in those tight shorts and sweater.

The plot of *The Court Jester*, such as it was, turned on Danny being required to remember, at a crucial point in the action, a certain rhyme. There were three goblets on a tray, two of which contained poison.

'The vessel with the pestle,' my brother began.

'The flagon with the dragon,' I added.

Neither of us could remember the third. 'Come on,' my brother said, and I could hear real anxiety – nothing must be forgotten, nothing – in his voice. 'Somebody. The third one.'

From the back of the car, in a voice so low at first I wasn't sure I had heard it, Mother said, 'the chalice with the palace.'

I let out a whoop and my brother kissed her and Mother repeated it again in a shy voice. 'The chalice with the palace is the brew that is true.'

At that instant we were all back in the Broadview, laughing until we cried, watching Danny in a ridiculous pair of tights, swinging to and fro on a rope in front of the castle wall, holding a tray in his hand, with the three glasses on it, shouting 'the vessel with the pestle, the flagon with the dragon, the chalice with the palace!' and not being able to remember which was the brew that was true.

When we got to the Cineplex, Miranda and I wanted to see an American picture, but my brother wanted to see a French film, shot in Provence with someone called Miou-Miou in it, which I thought was bound to be terrible, but I didn't want to start arguing with my brother and spoiling things for my mother, so we got seats down near the front, with Mother between my brother and me, and I took her hand and held it the way we used to. The picture was called *The Reader* and the title shots tracked down to a house, then to a window, then to a woman, sitting in warm light reading a book, all seen from an impossible and inhuman vantage point, like God's.

The image of the woman was getting bigger and bigger. Mother squeezed my hand and whispered: 'I don't like this at all.'

'What's the matter?' my brother whispered and Miranda said, 'Your mother is frightened.'

'Do you want to leave?'

'Oh yes,' my mother whispered.

'Why?'

'I don't know why.'

I got her up out of her seat and we fumbled our way to the exit over the other people's legs. I was thinking how all the good times in the movies were over for good and all, Charlie Chaplin, Buster Keaton and Mack Sennett, *Brief Encounter*, Bette Davis, Bogart, and Danny Kaye with your husband and your kids, and the whole story ends right here at the Odeon Cineplex, no more than two minutes into the running time, and the fact that your sons are beside you can't do a thing to stop your terror.

We got out into the light of day and returned her to the nursing home and that was the last time we ever took her out anywhere.

'She likes watching television,' my brother said, when the three of us were at the Chinese restaurant later, 'So why didn't she like the movie?'

I thought it must have something to do with the fact that she could take or leave the TV when it was on in the day room, but the movies were different, you had to give them your entire attention.

My brother said, 'It was the opening tracking shot, that long slow pan down from the sky right into the room where the woman was reading the book. That's what she couldn't take.'

I couldn't see what that had to do with it, but my brother told me he had read an anthropologist's account of showing films to primitive tribes in the 1920s. This indicated that if you were a Zulu or an Eskimo or someone who had never seen movies before, you might think: is the golden girl moving? Or am I? You might think this if you were a Zulu. You might also think it if your mind was giving way.

'Don't you see?' my brother said. 'She has forgotten the grammar of the cinema, how you go somewhere and sit in the dark and watch the golden girl growing larger and larger, all seen from the eye of God. No wonder she was frightened.'

'But,' I said, 'she remembered the chalice with the palace.'

'Because she remembers where she was and who she was with,' my brother said. 'What she can't remember is her relation to new images. She can't say, I am here in my seat, and this is just a film. It took her over completely.'

I remembered how my wife and I used to take our kids to the movies when they were small, and how when they saw a wolf bound across the screen at them, they shrieked and buried their heads in our laps. I could remember envying our children and thinking how diminished it was to be in control of the process of illusion.

Illness had returned my mother to the condition of my children. There was no distance, no membrane of knowing between her and the screen. She was, like them, defenceless before the wolf.

'What happened in the movie might be what is happening to her memory images,' my brother said. 'She sits in the movie theatre of her own mind and she doesn't know what these images are or what her relation to them is supposed to be. There's just one damned thing after another.'

I was thinking how crazy it must seem not to possess your own memories any more: the fire in the back pasture, and voices calling and the smell of cinders and a man in bathing trunks with a hose, none of it making sense because it no longer belonged to you, because you were no longer there, because you couldn't understand why these images were scrabbling across the white screen of your mind.

'No wonder she wanted to leave,' I said, thinking of my mother in the cinema of her mind, struggling to find the exit in the dark.

'I think she is fascinating,' my brother suddenly said. He

took a sip of Chinese tea and poured Miranda some and then, as if he was talking to himself, he said, 'The only people I can feel compassion for are people I find interesting.'

'Your mother too?' Miranda asked.

He nodded and then said, 'She's like a lab experiment . . . '

'In what?'

'In how much you can lose of yourself and still remain a human being,' he said briskly, looking at me as if I would understand. Miranda listened to the two of us, not touching her food. Then she eased her way out of the booth and said, 'You spend time with each other. I see you tomorrow.' I got up and followed her out, but she wouldn't come back and she wouldn't say what was bothering her.

'She doesn't like me,' my brother said when she had gone.

'She doesn't like the way we talk about Mother.'

'She's right.'

She didn't feel there was any place for her, between the two of us, sitting there in the booth of the Chinese restaurant, talking about the dividing line between compassion and pity. Every day of her life she had to live along that line, and she didn't want to discuss it.

When she had gone, I knew that I couldn't follow her, not that night anyway. My brother lit a cigarette and gazed at the carp in the fish tank behind the restaurant bar, and I felt as lonely as I had ever been in my life. My brother said he had to get back so I drove him to the airport and as he checked in, I asked him whether I could come down to stay with him for a couple of days.

'Right now?'

'Right now.'

'Is it as bad as that?'

I said it was.

On the flight, he turned to me and said, 'Do you know

why I feel good?' I didn't know why. 'Mother recognised me,' he said, taking a sip of whiskey. 'She still recognises me. I am a fifty-year-old man and the thing that matters most to me, the thing that actually makes me believe I exist, is the fact that an old woman in a nursing home still knows who the hell I am. Can you beat that?' He smiled, swirled the drink around, took a piece of ice in his mouth and crushed it between his teeth.

My brother's condominium was on the sixteenth floor of a tower overlooking the Charles River and from the windows you could see the long red snake of tail lights winding along the river parkway below. It was still too hot to sleep, and so we sat out on the balcony for an hour or two, drinking beer, while I told him how I wished I could get back with my wife and how I wished my children would forgive me.

Not having a wife or children of his own, my brother's reactions were unreadable, and I felt anguish at being unsure of his feelings. But he heard me out, and I sensed that he was listening and not judging. I must have talked for hours to that still shadow framed against the plate glass windows and the night sky.

Finally he said, 'I've got a clinic tomorrow.' He yawned and stretched and went in search of some sheets and pillows for the sofa bed. Then he went into his bedroom and closed the door. It was getting on for dawn, and the windows of the sitting room gave out on the whole view of Boston and the river and I didn't feel like going to sleep. I had said a few things I hadn't even thought before and I felt better for it.

I thought of my wife laughing and saying about my mother and the farm, 'She has a certain genius for discomfort.' Which was true. At the farm, there were no recliners or sofas with cushions where you could stretch out, just those hard-backed chairs around the fireplace.

Even my father worked on a straight-backed chair, without so much as a cushion to soften the cane seat. There was no virtue attached to all of this, no morality. It was more absent-mindedness than anything else.

I had never been in his apartment before, and I looked around, trying not to wake him, wondering whether it told me anything at all about what he was really like. The public part of it – the sitting room looking over the city – was gleaming and functional and, as my wife would have said, absent-mindedly uncomfortable. The private parts were a mess. In his study, Nettie's crimson fragment was hanging on the wall, beside his framed degrees, and against the wall by the desk stood Mother's unfinished picture of the three dark figures, where he had left it the night before when we got in from the airport. There were photographs of the two of us I had never seen crammed on to every available space on a cork bulletin board behind his desk. I didn't know how he could do any work with all those photographs watching him from his wall, but he obviously could because the desk itself was strewn with faxes and print-outs, business cards, post-it notes, journal reprints, file folders, paper-clips, pencils and styrofoam cups.

On the wall by the door were two light-boxes and when I flipped them on, a pair of brain scans lit up, the skull and the vertebrae in bright yellow, the brain sections in blue. The smoky outline of the jaw made me think of how a coastal shelf looks from an airplane, sloping down below you underneath the sea.

I was studying the scans, when I heard him come in.

'Find any clues?' he said. I turned around, feeling embarrassed. His apartment had taught me nothing about him, except how lonesome and silent his life must be in this cell high above the city.

'You've wiped the prints,' I said. 'What are these?'

'Nuclear magnetic resonance imaging, tracking the isotope methionine to show the cessation of protein synthesis in the right frontal and parietal lobes.'

He pointed at a dark region. 'There,' and then at another region, 'there. See the difference?'

When he pointed it out, I could see the inner diminution, the wasting away, and I wondered how it was that he managed to spend his life, so cool and self-possessed, in the midst of these images of loss.

He obviously liked showing me his work, because after breakfast he took me down to his lab at the teaching hospital. I can still remember the pleasure he took in treating me as if I were a student of his, and he was my teacher.

We are standing side by side, and I am looking down the eyepiece of an electron microscope. The cells on the glass slide – magnified six hundred times – are from the temporal lobe of a patient in her late sixties. The cells have been stained in order to highlight her neurons, axons and dendrites, the structural architecture of her brain. My brother is guiding me through these regions of inner space. The blurred brown oblongs are normal neurons. The dark blotches with long curving tails are called neurofibrillary tangles. At the centre of the image is a compacted black mass surrounded by a halo of inflammation. This is a deposit of amyloid protein, a form of scar tissue deep within this patient's brain. Under the microscope, it resembles a galactic storm, a starburst from an extinguished universe. When I say it looks beautiful, my brother says that everything becomes more beautiful the more closely you observe it.

Now take a look at this, my brother says, moving over to two shimmering images of the human brain, back lit by the light-box against the wall. The bone casing of the skull is outlined in purple, the cortex in light blue and the frontal lobes in red and yellow. This is positron emission tomography, my brother explains, and it enables neurologists to study brain function in real time. The subject is injected with radioactive glucose. The brain consumes glucose, and the more active a portion of brain, the more glucose it consumes. On the left-hand box, normal metabolic activity in the neurones of the healthy brain results in a symmetrical pattern of red areas in the left and right cerebral hemispheres. On the right-hand light-box, I see an irregular and shrunken pattern of darkish red which glows with the faintness of a dying ember. I am face to face with the neurophysiology of loss.

Look here, my brother says, picking up a DNA scan, an X-ray like transparency, which consists of columns of horizontal black and grey bars. One of these rows is the genetic fingerprint of the same patient, taken from a tiny smear of her blood. Notice the difference? my brother says, pointing to row six, her scan. I notice nothing. There, he says, pointing out the defect on the middle arm of chromosome 21. The cascade begins there, he says.

To my brother the word cascade means only the sequence of pathological effects, but for me the word has menace. I see a body tumbling down a black, liquid-filled shute. I catch him watching me. He raises his voice to bring me back to myself.

'The cascade begins when the genetic message governing the synthesis of protein leads to too much protein being produced or the failure of the enzymes to break the protein down. Do you follow me?'

I don't, but I nod just the same.

'The protein builds up into the scar-like deposits which destroy adjacent brain tissue and produce those dark matted coils and tangles on the slide.' My brother's methodical, neutral voice – the one he uses for his lectures – makes him sound like a stranger.

Being a neuropathologist, he says, is like joining a pool game in the middle, with the balls all over the baize and having to figure out where the balls were after the first shot. He touches the genetic fingerprint again. 'This is how we find the first shot.'

'So now we know,' I say.

'No, we are only at the beginning.'

There are bound to be other genetic defects involved, and doctors haven't tracked down more than a couple so far. Genetics can't be the whole story. What about the environment, I ask, irritated that I sound so respectful. Genetics, he says, simply gives us a certain predisposition to illness. The DNA is coded to trigger if we live a certain kind of life.

'What kind of life?'

'Wish we knew,' he says.

My brother isn't bothered by what he doesn't know. The answers will surrender themselves eventually. There is a serenity in his science which makes me envious and unhappy. 'I wish I knew how to change my life,' I say.

He acts as if he hasn't heard and counts off on his fingers the things science will be able to do for this kind of patient one day: implantation of DNA to correct the genetic defect; chemicals to retard production of protein; or chemicals to help the enzymes to break down and remove the protein; other chemicals to improve neurotransmitter function. Tragedy is thus transformed into a manageable condition.

'We'll get there,' he says.

'In time?'

He has his arm against my back, leading me out of the lab, switching off the lights behind him.

'We're two years from drug trials. Ten to fourteen years from prescription.' So there is hope, but not for this patient.

That is when it dawns on me who the patient is. It had to be against the rules, but then, the doctors are the ones who make the rules.

'I don't like looking at her like this,' I say, feeling that we have gone too far and have crossed some line of decency. He doesn't want to talk about it. He snaps off the light-boxes in the lab and leads me out into the street.

He said he had someone he wanted me to meet. 'A teacher,' he said, as we eased into the morning rush hour traffic on the cross-town expressway. 'Like you.'

The patient had come in with symptoms of numbness and pain in his muscles and joints. That was five years ago. He had ordered some tests, but they were just to be sure. He knew right away.

'Classic presentation. ALS.'

My brother spelled it out for me, 'Amyotrophic lateral sclerosis, also known as motor neurone disease.'

'Stephen Hawking's disease?'

My brother nodded. 'Radical and irreversible deterioration of the nerve centres responsible for muscular and autonomic function.'

It had never occurred to me before that my brother had to tell people they were going to die.

'How did you tell him?'

My brother signalled and pulled off the expressway ramp at the Charlestown exit and he said, 'I'm always giving people the good news. His name, by the way, is Moe.'

In the lobby of the St Mary's Extended Care Centre, the wheelchair cases are lined up against the walls; some are moaning, some intoning private mantras, some asleep with their mouths open, and some staring out at the heat shimmer above the lawn. Moe's room is near the lobby and his door is open.

Moe is lying on his side, facing a computer terminal and a printer, and there is a tube taped to the side of his pillow. My brother pats his arm in greeting and Moe gives a deep gargling sound by way of reply. I say hello and position myself in Moe's eyeline. He is a big man, with a full strong chest covered in dark curly black hair. His diminished thighs and legs lie concealed beneath a white sheet. He purses his lips round the tube and I can see his cheeks puffing out and his forehead wrinkling with effort. Slowly the words tap out on the computer screen: 'It is good of U to come.' The computer department at Moe's school had come up with the software and the hospital technical department had devised the straw and the keyboard. Moe can't move or talk but he can communicate with the world by blowing through a straw to activate the keyboard.

There are pictures of his wife and children on the walls, some of their drawings from school, a poster of a Greek Orthodox icon, and a sign saying, Nuclear Free Zone: No Enemas Here, and another one saying: If Choking or Gagging, Sit Me Upright.

I ask him what he thinks of his doctor, and Moe purses his lips together to send a message to the screen.

'He does what I tell him.'

Both of them grin. 'Any problems?' my brother asks and the nurse explains that he is having trouble with his bedsores. Moe blows into his straw. The word, 'Ouch!' comes up on the screen.

With an expert, gentle touch, my brother lifts the sheet and turns Moe over. His hip and his right shoulder are inflamed where his body weight presses him against the sheets. His legs are frighteningly thin and emaciated. While my brother is telling the nurses to change the bedsore ointment, Moe winks at me.

My brother leaves me to look in on another patient and

I tell him I wouldn't mind staying and talking to Moe for a while. Moe must think I am a strange kind of visitor, pressing into the domains of intimacy so quickly because I sit down on the bottom of the bed and ask him, right away, how much pain he is having. One by one, the words come up on the screen:

> 'i cant sit up because i cant hold my head up and to support it makes me gag. so my days are now spent lying on my side.
> there is no pain attributable directly to als although the deterioration of the organ in the brainstem which controls body temperature and frequent choking spells have led to some very traumatic moments. eating has become a hazardous occupation. as well my hips often hurt from lying that way.
> i have had much time to ponder and reflect and to try to understand what is happening. i write almost every day.
> it has been 4 years since i could hold a pen.'

It takes him many minutes to get this on to the screen and when he finishes he has to lie back and rest. Words matter to this man. Filling a screen with words is equal to a whole day's teaching in the classroom for me.

What I want to know is why he isn't more angry.

Letter by letter the words appear on the screen:

> 'i was angry for about three years. it ate me up. Then i stopped being angry. now i pray to jesus christ.'

I have no right to object to this, but I do, strenuously.

I tell him that I will not pray to someone who makes him suffer like this. His mischievous eyes do not lose their sense of humour. Letter by letter, more words emerge on the green screen.

> 'i lie here; i cannot move; however, i can listen, think, pray. how is it i feel love? and where is it coming from?'

I am sitting on his bed by this time, awkwardly laying my hand on his shoulder, wondering if he is able to feel it there.

I tell him it isn't my business to come all this way to try to turn him into an atheist. He smiles and then indicates his water bottle with his eyes. I help him drink his water through a straw. After that he goes to sleep almost immediately, his mouth open, his face blank with exhaustion.

His wife comes by, and we eat a sandwich in the corridor together while Moe is sleeping. She is a nurse herself with a full-time job and three kids to raise on her own, yet she manages to get down to the hospital every day to visit him. Five years spent in the company of illness have refined her pretty face into something grave and fine.

'Your brother has been good to Moe,' she says. 'Not like some of the other doctors.'

'Moe says my brother does what he tells him to.'

'It wasn't that way at the beginning, I can tell you. Your brother wanted Moe to do this and that, wanted him to fight this right down to the wire, and Moe went along for some time, and then I said, This is crazy, you know. We're talking about disease here, not some sports event, not some competition you can win or make a good showing in or anything like that. I think that woke Moe up some. He isn't like that any more.'

'Neither is my brother,' I say.

'I think he learned that from Moe. Accepting things.' She leaves and says I can stay until he wakes up again. When Moe comes to, I put my hand on his shoulder and say I had better be going. He makes one of those gargling sounds and I figure out that he wants the tube placed in his mouth. A word comes up on the screen.

'stay.'

When the nurses have changed his catheter and sponge-bathed his body, I ask him how he feels about the future. He doesn't seem to mind being asked. I put the tube between his lips and stand behind him to watch the words slowly come up on the screen.

> 'feel that i have to choose to live even now which is hard for someone so tired when i do this he takes care of meee mi fear and anxieti so hoping that i can be conscious for the move.'

'Conscious for the move.' The words glow on the screen and at first I don't understand them. Moe lies next to the screen, some of its green pallor reflected on his face, his eyes shut, the tube resting on his open lips.

Then I realise what he is trying to say. He wants to see everything, to feel everything, to hold on to his awareness of life until the very last moment; and to him this consciousness – whatever its desolation – is worth fighting for to the last instant. I have never met anyone before who values the ordinary state of human awareness so keenly.

It goes dark and the fluorescent lights come on overhead. A nurse comes in and puts a visor on Moe's forehead to shield him from the light and to allow him to see the computer screen better. I tell him he looks like the dealer at a crap game in a gangster movie. He smiles.

Then I ask him, as I might have asked a priest if I had one, what I should think about my mother's illness. His eyes remain shut for a long time, then his lips close around the tube and letter by letter, pause by pause, space by space, over twenty-five minutes, words begin to emerge onto the screen.

> 'consider the following now
> 1) illness. not the beginning of the end but the beginning of THE beginning. to be honest i did not FEEL this very strongly till about 6 months ago. nevertheless, i lived every day since my diagnosis to the fullest knowing the physical exertion would speed the progression of the illness. to sit back however, would have only robbed me of moments with my family and friends.
> thus, i continue. only now i sense if i had become a stoic or a fighter, i would probably be gone by now. rather, i face each day with a prayer. i try to be completely open to whatever christ brings.'

The word 'stoic' gives me the idea that he might have read my lecture. It made sense after all. I had sent it to my brother, though he'd never told me what he thought about it. While Moe is having another rest, I get talking to one of the nurses and she tells me that my brother had come in one day and plastered some sheets all around the room – because Moe couldn't hold anything in his hand – and then my brother got the nurses to wheel Moe's bed round from sheet to sheet so that he could read the whole lecture. I feel ridiculously pleased, as if all the shame attendant upon that lecture had suddenly been wiped away.

When Moe wakes up, I tell him how angry the lecture had made my wife. Up on the screen come the words,

> 'anger is a waste of time.'

I tell him that a friend of mine once said you don't get any smarter or wiser as you get older. All that happens is that you understand the true meaning of clichés. Like: 'Take it day by day'. Or 'As long as you've got your health'. Or that cliché about anger: 'You can't get beyond it, until you've gone through it.' Words come up quickly on the screen,

> 'so get through it.'

I ask him what he thought about my lecture. His answer takes twenty minutes to appear on the screen. More and more often he has to stop and rest.

> 'better to know and grow from the experience than to remain aloof and have no basis for wisdom. stoicism. not much of a motivator. perhaps the unsung reason for searching out one's spirituality.'

'Not much of a motivator.' It had turned out that I wasn't much into stoicism either, whatever I had said in that lecture. I was more of a rage rage type, actually. He winks when I say that.

I stroke his shoulder and want to say, though I can't get it right, that what I had learned from him and from Mother was that when you strip us right down, when illness pares us back to our core, we remain creatures of the word. Nothing can save us but the word, the messages we send from deep in the shaft of sickness.

Letters came up very slowly, one by one, on the screen.

'believe in the word.'

I tell him that my father had said she was on a voyage away from us, and that there were times when we all wished we could follow her. She couldn't tell us what it was like, I say, but you can.

'a journey, yes.'

It takes minutes for him to get it down, his face sweating with the effort. I can hardly bear to watch.

'away from my body away from family and the world I know,'

I walk up and down the room, so I won't have to look, feeling ashamed of the effortlessness of my own body and my speech, while he lies there underneath a sheet in a darkened room, struggling to report back from unvisitable terrain:

'into the heart of life.'

I can't ask any more of him. He lies still, eyes shut, beneath his visor, sweating, emaciated, exhausted. I want to thank him, but it seems altogether too lightweight a gesture to do that, as if I had come for advice or a consultation or something, so I just say goodbye and stroke his inert arm again and add, 'we're not finished with each other,' feeling foolish that I have said it. A thin, tired cry issues from his throat.

A nurse comes in and sends a command to the printer which prints out his part of our conversation. As I leave, I turn back. The computer screen is glowing green and empty. Before it lies a big tapering shape under a sheet, framed between the steel bars of a hospital bed. The green visor is still shading his eyes but he is asleep.

In a cab on the way back to my brother's place, I unroll the computer paper and discover that, at the end of what he had said to me, the nurse had printed out a poem of his:

> *5NO*
> what is happening?
> what are these flashes crashing noiselessly from side
> to side in my mind? spells of brownouts follow
> ozone cinders down the unknown path
> the child within calls out how much farther, dad?

When I got back to my brother's place, he was sitting in a pool of light at the table, eating dinner. The glow of the city rose over the horizon and above that there was a sky full of stars. He was wearing a dressing gown over a T-shirt and sweat pants, and in that dressing gown, in the pool of light, he looked solitary and grand, like some abbot in a mountain monastery. 'I kept some for you,' he said, and we ate the rest of his Indian take-out together. When I told him I had spent the whole day with Moe, he said, 'I figured you might.' I asked him how long he gave him.

'Three months, maybe four at the outside.'

'Does he know?'

'Of course.'

I wondered about friendship between a doctor and a patient, between a man who knows what it is like to die, second by second, and another man who knows everything about that death – down to the molecular structure of cell decay – except what it feels like. He knew the meaning of those dark regions of Mother's scans, the hidden logic of the sequence of numbers in her test scores. What he didn't know was what it was like to be her. It struck me then that his science was the form of love he understood best.

I was thinking about this when he said, 'ALS accelerates if you move; slows down if you keep still. Every time Moe communicates it speeds up the deterioration. Further proof, if need there be, for the existence of a merciful creator – as I always say to Moe.'

'And what does Moe say to that?'

'He says mind your own damned business.'

My brother pushed back his chair. 'I use Moe in my medical ethics classes. I ask them whether a certain neurologist is entitled to allow an ALS patient to hook up to a computer system, if the doctor knows that using it will shorten the patient's life.'

'So why did you?'

My brother gave a small laugh. 'My students always say the doctor shouldn't. Then I take them to meet Moe. He changes their minds in half an hour. What conclusion do we draw? I ask them.'

'Speech can matter more than life itself,' I said.

'Exactly,' my brother said and lit a cigarette. 'The word. Believe in the word.'

My brother cleared away the boxes of take-out and went to the fridge and got out a beer for each of us.

'I also give my class a thought experiment. If you had to choose, which would you prefer: to lose your mind but keep your body, or to lose your body but keep your mind?'

'I don't like games like that,' I said.

'Thought experiments.'

'I don't care what the hell they're called.'

He ignored me. 'Asking this question is a way of exploring the value human beings place on self-awareness.'

'It's voyeuristic,' I said.

'Come on,' he said, 'We're all moral tourists here. Illness is another country. None of us has any idea. That's what thought experiments are for. My students, by the way, are all sure. Until they meet Moe.'

'And then?'

'He tells them about the choking spells or watching his legs wasting away, and then,' my brother smiled, 'they're not so sure. He's great with students.'

'You must make a hell of a team,' I said.

My brother went over and sat on the sofa. 'Mother can only suffer. She can't give her experience any meaning. That's the worst thing about it for her.'

I didn't know why he was so sure about this, but I let him go on.

'Moe, on the other hand, can shape his experience. He sees it in a Christian light – which I can't stand – but that is what keeps him holding on. I nearly counted him out twice before this, you know. Respiratory infections. Each time he pulls himself back from the edge.'

'Positive mental attitude,' I said. I didn't know what name to give to that fierce thing which made Moe refuse his fate, but whatever its name, even desperation, it was life, and my 'stoicism' now seemed to me nothing more than surrender.

My brother walked across the darkened room and

stood looking out at the blue lights of the runways at Logan. 'I used to think, because of Mother, that consciousness was the most precious thing of all, and oblivion the thing to be resisted at all costs. Now I'm not so sure. Now I see what Moe is going through, how he sees his own linguistic powers disintegrating, his own words and sentences unravelling on the screen. I'm not so sure I could stand it.'

I wasn't sure why he was telling me all this, but I was glad he was. Finally he said, 'It's all a question of how much awareness a human being can stand.' He glanced back at me from the window, 'I know what you think, but believe me, it's good that Mother doesn't know.'

'She's still suffering. It's not over. She still knows what's happening.'

'Sure?' he said.

'Sure,' I said. 'After all, she still recognises you. As long as she does, she can still suffer.'

I wanted to tell my brother about the night when I had lain beside my mother in the dark and watched her sleep, lying on her back with her mouth open, how I had imagined taking the pillow and holding it over her face. I wanted to confess the shame of that to someone, to unburden myself of that memory and the rage it contained. Then, just as quickly as those feelings came over me again, I found myself thinking how absurd they were. Why had I ever wanted to do such a thing? Her awareness, that fragile and damaged thing, suddenly seemed infinitely precious to me, like a painted egg I might have crushed in my hands and now saw for the thing that it was.

I didn't say any of this to my brother. Instead I told him about an evening a few nights before when Mother and I had been sitting there in her room, watching the people waiting at the bus-stop in the rain opposite her window, and she had seemed faded and blurred and ebbing away, and I told her that I felt like going down to Boston to pay him a visit. Out of the stillness of the room, she said, 'I see him.'

'What do you see?'

Long pause. She looked me straight in the eye.

'I see him walking through the gates of truth.'

My brother went still. I knew he could see himself as she saw him: a small child, between two ruined columns reaching up into the sky, among the flames and smoke of some great destruction, a child frozen between the weight of the columns, unable to move, within the gates of truth. I knew he saw her – as I did – standing on the other side of the gates, beckoning us both to follow.

ON THE FLIGHT back from Boston, I rehearsed what I wanted to tell my wife, and when I made the call from the airport arrival lounge I tried to imagine her listening to me, by the refrigerator door in our kitchen, with the cool of it against her back, while she smoked a cigarette and ran a hand through her hair. But we hadn't spoken for six months, and I couldn't picture how she might be or what she was thinking.

'Hi, it's me.'

She listened and then said gently, 'Why are you calling?'

I had the uncanny feeling that I knew why I was calling but not whom I was calling. So I tried to explain that I had done a lot of thinking and had been down staying with my brother and could we see each other.

She let out a breath of cigarette smoke.

'Where are you? There's all this noise. Are you all right?'

'I'm OK. I want to see you.'

'What for?'

'Just to see what would happen.'

She changed the subject: 'I went to see your mother.'

I said, 'Why?'

'I loved your mother.'

'Why are you telling me this?'

'She didn't know who I was.'

'You can't tell.'

'I could tell.' Then she said, 'I know how you must feel.'

Perhaps it was her way of saying she too had been

thinking, her way of moving towards me. It was one of those phone calls which could have changed everything. I said I wanted to see her right away.

'Maybe we shouldn't.'

'Why not?'

'Not sure, just thinking.'

'What about?'

'Where we go from here.'

'That depends on us.'

'But look at what happened,' she said. 'I still don't get it.'

'Me neither,' I said, trying to make it sound funny.

'You should be the one who does.'

'But I don't. I had to do it, but I'm not saying I understand all the reasons why.'

'You've got to do better than that.'

I see now, as I play it back for the fiftieth time, the words that might have turned it in the right direction. But at the time, on the airport telephone, I didn't have any words at all. So I changed the subject. I said I wanted to bring my daughter to the nursing home, because I thought my mother might be able to draw her. My wife listened and said she didn't think it was a good idea.

I could have spent another couple of minutes, trying to get her to reconsider, but I didn't want to. So I hung up.

I knew that from my wife's point of view, the problem was my whole existence, my lunatic devotion, my every afternoon and evening at the nursing home. I could even sympathise with her point of view. Who would want their children mixed up with that? So instead of my daughter, it ended up with me and my mother in the day room downstairs, surrounded by big pieces of coloured paper and crayons, drawing like schoolchildren side by side. I drew a house, as I always seem to do, a house with smoke coming out of the chimney, and four people peering out of the windows anxiously as if they were watching the sky for enemy planes. It was all in the nature of an experiment. The only piece of work I had done in the year since my father had died had been to start an essay about the case of Willem de Kooning, which I had followed in the specialist art journals. At the end of his life, Kooning suffered from dementia, was unable to recognise anyone or speak, yet he continued to paint. The question was: did these paintings deserve to be called art?

THE CASE OF WILLEM DE KOONING

> . . . The work de Kooning produced from within dementia has divided the critics. Some believe the later work displays a surer line and firmer grasp of colour than those which he completed in a preceding period when he was often drunk. The new paintings are composed of swirls of colour, so unworldly, so unlike anything seen in nature, so unlike the works of conscious intention that other critics have argued they are valueless as works of art, merely of interest to neurologists and clinicians. Yet it is surely a mistake to restrict the definition of art to those works which are the product of conscious intention. The whole direction of twentieth century art has been away from conscious intention towards unleashing the spontaneous, infantile and subconscious sources of creative energy . . .
>
> De Kooning's work raises the possibility that art might still exist where there is no artist; that a painting might still be painted where there is no self to do the painting. The illness might merely be paring away the reflexive, self-aware and cognitive

capacities of the brain, leaving behind deep structures, either genetically inherited or formed in earliest infancy, which could continue to respond to the elemental geometry of colour and line. If this were true, de Kooning's brush might no longer be connected to an intentional self, but rather to the deep structures of his own creative inspiration. The argument about de Kooning thus is not just about the relation between inspiration and illness. It is also a rerunning of a much more ancient argument about the nature of art itself. On one side, the romantic account of creativity, as the work of raw, unmediated feeling. On the other the classical account, which locates artistic creativity in the reflexive and self-aware portions of the brain . . .

The de Kooning case raises another troubling problem: whether the painter, sane, might have actually wished to embrace the state of mind of de Kooning – lost and demented; whether, it might even be said, that de Kooning had sought or at least welcomed his final destitution. This hypothesis might appear absurd, were it not for the frequency with which de Kooning, at the height of his fame, insisted that his creative life was one long struggle to escape his conscious, intentional self and return to the primary impulses of artistic inspiration. Consider, for example, this quotation from de Kooning, at the height of his fame in the mid 1950s:

'Y'know the real world, this so-called real world, is just something you put up with, like everybody else. I'm in my element when I am a little bit out of this world: then I'm in the real world – I'm on the beam. Because when I'm falling I'm doing all right; when

I'm slipping. I say, hey this is interesting! It's when I'm standing upright that it bothers me: I'm not doing so good; I'm stiff. As a matter of fact, I'm really slipping most of the time, into that glimpse. I'm like a slipping glimpser.'

At the time, I could write about de Kooning, of course, but not a word about my mother. I was using prose the way builders use scaffolding on a derelict building – to keep it from falling into the street.

Mother had always admired de Kooning's work of the early 1950s. I remember going to see a de Kooning retrospective with her and wondering what she saw in these strange pictures whose surfaces seemed so violent and childish and when you looked closer, turned out to be as carefully composed as a Rembrandt self-portrait. I learned to appreciate de Kooning's paintings from watching my mother circle round them with an intense, melancholy respect. She had stopped painting by then and as she looked at the canvases, it was as if she were realising what she would have had to abandon – certainly all of us, perhaps herself as well – if she had wanted to get to the wild and exalted place de Kooning had reached.

Sitting beside my mother in the day room, I finished my drawing of the house, hoping that I could pull her into the rhythm of what I wanted to do. She drew a house too, like mine, the walls a little more slanted, the angles a little more crooked than mine, but still a house, with smoke curling up from a chimney and two flowers on either side of a red door. When she finished it, she surveyed it as if it had been done by someone else.

'Mother, will you draw me?'

I put the charcoal into her left hand and I put a fresh sheet of paper down, and I sat there holding her right hand, posing so that she would understand what was wanted of her.

For a moment, she remained motionless, not looking at the pencil or the paper, just smiling faintly. Then, as if the pencil placed between her fingers and my expectant face triggered a forgotten power and a forgotten scene, she began to draw. The first charcoal line appeared. Her eyes rose to take in the fall of my eybrows, my jaw and the shape of my head. She brought her free hand up towards my face, as if to estimate distance and proportion and shape. I sat still, thinking of the light streaming through her eyes to her visual cortex, transferred there into a chemistry of signals moving along neurochemical pathways to the brain centres controlling her hand and eye co-ordination, and then into the muscles governing her left hand as it drew my face out of the whiteness of the paper. I was in the presence of the mystery of vision, studied since men and women first questioned their own capacities, a mystery still not understood, happening here and now before me. It was as if she were suddenly a transparent figure and I could see within her to the secret chemistry of art, to the neurological impulses that had made her able to paint, as no one else ever had, the true likeness of myself. In the nursing home day room, at the art desks, our knees touching, I believed that there were some losses that could be made good, some attempts at recapitulation in time that could succeed, if the will was sufficiently tenacious.

Then just as quietly as she began, my mother stopped. The charcoal remained in her hand, poised above the last line, but it would move no further. Such connection as had been made was now broken and my mother stared off once again into space. I took the charcoal out of her hand and I said, 'Thank you.' She didn't say anything.

It was a good likeness. A long, thin face with big ears and indecisive eyes stared back at me. The lines were firm, accurate and graceful. The primary capacity, her first language, had survived all damage.

Yet the hand that had been drawing was disconnected from intentions and feelings. The sketch might have been done by a machine. There was no way to tell that the person depicted was a son and the artist his mother. There was a disconnection between her and me and between her hand and herself. Her primary language, the language of her hand and eye, was intact, yet it was floating loose inside her mind, like some piece of satellite debris tumbling over and over in space. She put the charcoal down and folded her hands in her lap.

'Go home now,' she said.

> Where does art come from? From the intentional self or from the primal self? Willem de Kooning kept painting after he ceased to be able to speak or reason or recognise those closest to him. The romantic view of art connects the painter's brush to the primal self; the classical view to the intentional self. What happens when one is sheared away from the other?

I told Miranda it wasn't her fault, but I felt ashamed of having been with her. Not shame about her, but about myself. I should have been ashamed to be with anyone. I felt I had been a drowning man and she had pulled me out of the water and I would always be grateful to her, but that it wasn't right to continue. She had been good to me, but it did nothing to end my shame, my sense of not having stood through this on my own two feet. She couldn't help me, and she always knew she couldn't – which was the best thing about her – but now I had to find my own way forward, without her.

'I wasn't helping you,' she said. 'I wasn't even trying to help you.'

'I know that.'

'I was with you. That was all. Just with you.'

'I know.'

'Why don't you understand?'

I got up to collect some things I kept in her cupboard. Like a child, I wanted to vanish and for every trace of me in this apartment to disappear as if it had never been.

She said she had felt me slipping away from her and hadn't known what to do about it. She felt that when I went down to Boston to be with my brother she had lost me for good.

'So why?'

I said I didn't know why. Something had clarified itself, yet I felt absurd to be so inarticulate, my face numb and my voice colourless. She said she was going to get herself transferred to another of the homes run by the same company, and I said that was a good idea.

Then, for the first time, I felt all her anger, all the resentment of having helped me and having got so little in return, so little of the understanding that I prized in her but had shown so little of myself. She turned her back on me and walked over to the window and said, over her shoulder, 'In Mindanao they say a man like you is . . . '

'What?' I said

'Nothing.' She crossed her arms and stayed with her back turned until I had shut the door behind me. I never did learn what kind of man they called me in Mindanao.

I NOW SPENT EVERY morning with my mother before going off to teach my classes and every evening as well, though by then she was in her wheelchair and I was the only person who could understand what she was saying.

'She gone gospedal.'

'Really? I didn't know that. Who's gone to the hospital?'

'Gospedal Shirley.'

'But you haven't seen Shirley since you were a little girl.'

She laughs, cunning, sly. 'Shirley lost the shirt.'

'I don't think so.'

'Yes, Shirley . . . '

'What did Shirley do?'

Long pause. 'Who?'

Then she would look out of the window and say,

'It is . . . boscon . . . '

'What has gone?'

'Boscon,' she would repeat, as if I hadn't understood anything.

'Boston. My brother is in Boston.'

She shook her head, as if to say,

'You're not paying attention.'

'OK. Right, Boscon not Boston. So boscon who?'

'No, no, no . . . ' She shakes her head. It is no use. 'He is in vazal.'

Go along with this, you think. Let her take you where she wants to.

'Do you think so?'

'Yes,' she says, and you are sure she is talking about Father.

'Father is dead.'

She nods. 'Pebbles,' is what she says.

Yes, there were pebbles. Round, flinty pebbles and moist brown earth, piled high all round the coffin. Yes, Mother, pebbles.

She shakes her head. No, no, not that way.

'I want my boy.'

'I am your boy.'

'Why is a boy gone?'

'He's not gone, he's here.'

'Boy gone, gone, gone. Going, going . . . '

'Gone.' Laughter.

'I can't stand this.' She smiles, almost laughs.

'Mother?'

'I can't stand . . . this.'

'I can't stand it either.' I put my head on her shoulder and I hear her heart beating in the arteries in her neck.

Lunatic conversations by the hour, she looking at me, as if to say, 'Am I making sense?' And me encouraging her to go on, even though I didn't know what she was talking about. Her speech reminded me of a film I saw on television once about some travellers lost in the desert, who try to attract the attention of passing planes by reflecting the light of the sun with a piece of broken mirror.

'I am pizner.'

'Prisoner?'

'Pizner.'

'Oh no, you're not.'

'I will run away.'

'Oh no, you won't.'

'Into the road.'

'No.'

'Into the field.'

'No.'

'Into the . . . '

'Where?'

'The ground.' A hard, bright smile flashes across her face.

First syntax and word order, then the words themselves – the serifs, the letters, the endings – eroding like the sandstone decorations of an ancient building lashed by the wind.

'Let's go for a walk.'

'Where?'

'Down to the end of the hall.'

'Who does that?'

'We do.'

'Why we?'

'What else is there?'

One weekend my brother came up, and he sat and watched me feeding her dinner, one forkful of chicken à la king at a time, followed by one spoonful of jello at a time, then holding the glass for her so she wouldn't spill it down the green bib round her neck. She was so hunched over by then that it wasn't easy getting the spoon in her mouth, and she couldn't eat anything that required much chewing because they had taken the plate out of her mouth so she wouldn't swallow it by mistake. She let you kiss her, or hold her hand, but she was so bent she couldn't see your face unless you got down on your knees beside her chair. My brother watched her and me and didn't say anything.

After the nurses led her back upstairs, I didn't want to take him back to my place so we went into the chapel room, where memorial services for former patients were held and he said, immediately, 'What's the point?'

'Of what?'

'Of visiting.'

'Why not?'

'Is there anything left?'
'How much do you need for it to be worthwhile?'
'I need something.'
'OK. Let's review the evidence. What you're asking is "is this a person or is this a vegetable?" '
'Come on, I didn't mean that.'
'I would say she is. Definitely. She has personhood. She has the habits a person has. If you say the word coffee, she says "Cawfee", in imitation of Peg Lawson in Alton. That's the habit of a person. You couldn't mistake the way she does that imitation for anybody else on earth. So that's number one. We have personhood.'
'Let's stop this.'
'No, it's a good question: what exactly are we doing here? So let's figure it out. Miranda used to say, "She sure is a character." Do you know what that meant? It meant she hit you if you tried to take off her sweater without her permission.'
My brother sat down and listened, with a look of pity on his face that made me so angry I had to turn away.
'Have you looked at her hands recently? Of course you haven't. She has calluses on the inside of the left thumb and right side of her index finger. Know why? Until her fall, until she had to go into the wheelchair, she used to walk six hours a day, from the nursing station to the picture window overlooking the back garden, up and down, till that guard rail had worked a groove right into her hand. Imagine the determination in all that walking. Imagine what it takes. That's what I call a person. That's what I call a character. What do you think, Doctor? What do we call that? Walking your blues away?'
My brother wouldn't say anything.
'You could say these things signify. You could say that journeying back and forth from the nursing station to the

fire escape door, a hundred times a day, was a voyage with a purpose in mind. On the other hand, you could say it means nothing at all. Is this magical thinking? Is this just a lie to keep myself going? Come on, tell me.'

'We better stop this,' my brother said.

But nothing was going to stop this. 'Perhaps it's just disinhibition. Maybe she's just disinhibiting. Maybe we're just on automatic pilot here.'

'I never said that.'

I ignored him. 'Sometimes she laughs. Sometimes the pills go flying, or the mashed potatoes end up on Jackie Tatham's face opposite her at the lunch table, or Mrs Yang begins pissing in the shower, and she sees all this, and she just begins laughing. And I laugh too. Because it's funny as hell in here. It really is.'

He was staring at me, willing me to stop, but I was not going to. 'Does she have a self? Isn't that what you want to know? It's what my students want to know. I could write a book about this. Does she have thoughts about her thoughts? Does she have second order desires?'

'For Christ's sake, stop talking like this. I said one thing, and you've gone crazy.'

'Oh no, I haven't. Just sit there and shut up till I have finished.' He sat there, looking at his hands.

'What kind of a self are we talking about? A couple of months ago, I was lying beside her on the bed in her room and I asked her, "Are you ever sad?" And right away, staring up at the ceiling, she said, "Oh yes."

'That's a second order thought. You look around the yellow room and the walls and the ceiling and the linoleum and you think to yourself, 'What kind of a life is this?'

'But the circuits are going down. Every day I come in here and one more has gone. She could walk three months ago. She could eat her food three months ago. She could talk. Now the words are going and everything she says is blurred like the words in a kid's writing book left out in the rain.

'Last week I came in, she was sitting on the floor, with blood on her face and a tooth in her hand, and she didn't even know it was her tooth. Her leg was at this crazy, terrible angle, and she didn't even know. So this is where we are. Isn't it interesting?'

My brother got up and came towards me.

'She has left her self behind. I sit with her, looking out of the window at the Korean Church next door and the minutes go by, and I think: What's so good about a self? What do you need it for? Those streetcars are very far away. Look, Mother, that man on the park bench, he is on another planet. Look, Mother, look, a starling is drinking in the puddle on the roof. Look . . . '

I couldn't follow the thread any more. All I knew was that I was standing there in the middle of the chapel room, and my brother was holding me in his arms, tight and stiff as men do when they aren't used to it, holding me so I would stop, so I wouldn't go any further, so I could come back to myself.

AROUND THIS TIME, I was teaching a course called 'Philosophy and Shakespeare', but which was devoted almost entirely to *King Lear*. It took my students by surprise that I force-marched them through every line before we came to themes and philosophical arguments. I even made them learn the big speeches by heart, as if they were in high school. In retrospect, I taught the course as if I was in the grip of some large fury, at their shallowness and insubstantiality, as well as my own. I thought: Once in your lives, you're going to be shown something that leaves you speechless, something that makes you respect the word as if it were holy. We are going to take these scenes to pieces and at the end of it, you still won't know how it was done. I wanted something very badly from that experience. I would call it redemption, except that I don't believe redemption is possible.

We would get to Act IV where the mad king, asleep in Cordelia's tent under the surgeon's care, slowly wakes to the sight of his daughter and his trusted Kent. There is nothing in literature, I would say, which describes more accurately the complex processes implicit in the apparently simple act of recognising a human face. The waking king whispers:

> Pray, do not mock me:
> I am a very foolish fond old man,
> Fourscore and upward, not an hour more or less;

To deal plainly,
I fear I am not in my perfect mind.
Methinks I should know you and know this man;
Yet I am doubtful: for I am mainly ignorant
What place this is, and all the skill I have
Remembers not these garments; nor I know not
Where I did lodge last night. Do not laugh at me;
For, as I am a man, I think this lady
To be my child . . .

Methinks I should know you

People kept asking me: does she recognise you? As if recognition is simple, binary, yes or no. Actually, she was simultaneously aware that she should recognise me and yet sometimes unable to do so. This shows, I would tell my undergraduates, that the visual cortex relays messages which the processing centres are unable to recognise. Vision and recognition must be distinct capacities, as are thinking and knowing.

By this stage, I was all in pieces inside her; name, face, texture of skin, shape of my eyes, all tumbling over and over in the darkness of her mind. Upon occasion, she could catch a piece of the broken mirror and hold it long enough to know who I was. Then that shard would slip loose and sink back into the shadows and she wouldn't give a flicker of recognition.

Sometimes she looked sly and knowing. Then I would think, she isn't forgetting. She is pushing me away. She has locked me out. She means to do this. It was like standing outside the lighted windows of my wife's house, wishing that she would come out and take me in.

It was as my brother had said: if she failed to recognise you, you ceased to exist. No longer her son, no longer anyone. Acknowledge that I exist. Acknowledge your son.

And she did. Eventually. A delay opened up between vision and recognition. I told my brother about this and he explained that the processing centres were taking longer and longer to find us. She knew we were there, but she didn't know where. The brain, he said, appears to have some capacity to re-wire itself, to channel functions out of scarred zones into healthy ones. Not all areas of the brain are operative: apparently empty rooms are kept in waiting, ready for emergencies. She hid her memories of me in these rooms in the hope that disease might not find them, my name in one room, the memory of my face in another, the sound of my voice in a small closet at the end of the corridor. But the disease was thorough. It tracked down her memory, room by room, snuffing out each synaptic spark.

Not only was she ceasing to recognise her sons, she was ceasing to recognise herself. Or to say it another way, she could only recognise her sons if she could first recognise herself as our mother.

Look, I would tell my class, the mad king at first does not recognise his daughter, because he does not recognise himself. I never saw a performance of the play which managed to express the relation between losing yourself and losing everyone else. I had to act it out for them myself, in the middle of the class: the way the king pats his own body, running his hand over the hospital garments they have put on him. I would be up there in the middle of a class of undergraduates, patting my old tweed jacket, running my hands across my own arms, and I would see them looking at me, as my children did after the break-up of my marriage, asking themselves: Who is this? Why is he like this?

Who am I? he wonders. All that has survived from his passage across the heath is a virtual self, an after-image of the kind that lingers before your eyes after a flashgun has gone off.

All the skill I have remembers not these garments.

Selfhood is in the garments, I would tell my class, in the raiment of a king, in the crown whose remembered imprint he may still faintly feel on his brow.

He slowly comes back to himself. He remembers it now. He was a king. She was his daughter.

She couldn't have said my name, she couldn't have said I was her son but she knew who I was. I knew. Take my hand. Turn it over. Look at the lines. Look how they fit into each other. Look how alike our hands have become. A man's hand, a woman's hand, becoming alike in time. No rings now, not the wedding band, nothing but what we share. Age is claiming both of our hands now, hers and mine. She looks at them. She is thinking: Whose hands are these?

The king lifts his hand towards his daughter. Think, I tell my class, of the way infants grab a finger when it is extended to them. This is the primary identification process: the elementary awareness of an otherness to be reached for and held.

At the end she recognised me as an infant recognises its mother. When she was bedridden and unable to speak, I could extend a finger close to her hand, and she would reach up and take it.

Then an evening came, like thousands before it, when I entered her room and she was lying in bed, with her hands upon the covers, her ancient face lit by the bedside lamp, and she turned slowly at the sound of my footsteps and looked at me. I stood still and her gaze continued, clear, focused and entirely indifferent. Then she looked away. This time I was sure that she neither knew nor cared who I was. I stood in the doorway, while she looked away, and I remembered the night I had been with my wife on the hillside and how the farm in the distance had looked like the *Andrea Doria*, that ship going down through the ocean, with its lights left on, blazing through the dark. The eyes that do not see, the eyes that have no memory, the eyes that are dead. I had arrived at the moment, long foretold, hopelessly prepared for, when Mother took the step beyond her self and moved into the world of death with her eyes open.

In her life she managed to teach us what it was like, in this realm beyond speech. She had done what she could to take our fear of it away, to take it upon herself, so we would not be frightened when our turn came. It was as if she was always saying to us: Look, it is only this, only this. I have been there. Only this.

There was never a single moment in which the illness showed her any mercy, never a moment when it let her be. For at the end, it came with epilepsy, which sent huge juddering tremors through her exhausted body, which caused her to bite her tongue and bleed, and which left her, afterwards, spent and exhausted, taking long, agonising breaths from the depths of her being. To this day, I hear that sound.

When she slept my brother and I talked, side by side, at her bed, looking at her ancient face, wondering whether she would wake. That was when he said, looking at her on her back with her mouth open, 'I always wondered why she stopped painting. She shouldn't have. It might have saved her.'

It was no longer a betrayal to tell him our secret. He had been away at college at the time, and Father was away at a convention, and I was alone with her at the farm.

She is wearing her painting things; they always made her look years younger, as if she were back in art school, still safe from what life has in store for her. She has been painting in the studio and she comes back into the kitchen and takes a cup of coffee out on to the porch. She sits down to drink it on one of the green canvas chairs and stares out at the smoky line of the low hills in the distance. Then she stands up and says, 'Come back to the studio with me.'

Stacked against the walls, with their faces turned away, are perhaps fifteen of her canvases and several marbled cardboard portfolios of her drawings. She begins mixing paint and invites me to join her. First one Windsor & Newton tube, then another, then another, are squeezed on to the palette.

'Do you really want me to be doing this?' I say in a voice that tries not to sound scared.

She nods and hums to herself and watches me, until every single tube of paint has been emptied, and the floor is littered with the lead husks of empty tubes.

'Now mix it all up,' she says, and hands me the thickest brush she has. Blues and greens, reds, oranges, siennas, yellows, whites, cobalt blues, Prussian blues, night blacks all bleed together, losing themselves, in a viscous, oily paste, the colour of despair.

Quietly, she turns the canvases over, one by one.

'Now paint,' she says.

I am holding the large brush, pregnant with paint, and I do not know whether I should.

'Do it,' she repeats. She does not stay to watch. She

walks out into the orchard and leaves me alone. I know I have no choice.

First a landscape. Then an Alton front door. The Japanese maple against a dusk sky. Four separate studies of the house. An unfinished sketch of mountains. An unfinished portrait of my father. Three studies of thistles.

Soon every canvas against the wall is daubed. In half an hour, I cover over her life's work.

'There,' she says, for she has come back when I have finished the last one, 'that's over with.'

Only one painting, the one on the easel, had been put aside, out of harm's way: the study of the two figures who seem to be beckoning to the third in the foreground.

She locks the door behind her, washes her hands with turpentine, throws her painting things away and never paints another picture in her life.

'How could you?' my brother said, when I had finished.

I took my mother's hand, the bones and the black veins visible beneath the sere envelope of skin.

I had assisted at a scene of mutilation, like the mourning rituals of countries where widows cut and daub their own garments and beat their temples in sorrow.

Only she couldn't bear to do the mutilation herself, so she had me do it for her. I was faithful. I was true. I did what I was told.

'Why?' my brother whispered.

She was so calm, so cheerful. No rage, no fury, nothing, just that strange, off-key humming of hers, that inner song only she could hear.

If it was mutilation, then what possessed her to do it? Was it just the dawning consciousness of failure, the moment when a proud woman looked at her work and knew that she lacked the final measure of courage to get where she wanted to go? She hated the second-rate, all excuses.

'Remember how she was with us? She was charitable when we failed at something, but she never called it anything else but failure.'

'I can't stand it that she gave up. I can't.'

'Not giving up. Just letting go,' I said. 'Like Moe said.'

'But she was there. She had it in her hands, such pleasure. She was good. Why didn't she know it was there?' He said this as if everything he was ever going to do in his own life turned on why she had stopped painting, as if he feared that her final gesture was a fate which might one day become his own.

I didn't see it that way. I thought she had looked deep inside herself and had suddenly realised, one summer morning, that she would never have what she needed. Now that I am as old as she was then, I see that it takes courage to surrender, to know the difference between giving up and giving in.

My brother said, 'I always thought that last picture was her way of looking at this, at what was coming for her. And she couldn't stand it and that was why she stopped. Two figures beckoning for her to follow.'

Perhaps it was her surrender to the dying that is in all our cells from the beginning. Perhaps she chose to make her peace with it early, given that she knew, not merely how she would die, but that she would lose the memory that she had ever painted any pictures at all.

I can see her, striding up and down the studio in her bare feet, in her jeans and the white shirt tied about her waist, a bottle of beer in her hand, held by the lip. She is humming softly to herself,

It's still the same old story.
The fight for love and glory
A case of do or die . . .

We were beside her now, holding her hands on either side of the bed and her eyes were closed and her breathing was slow and agonised and rasping, and her cheeks had collapsed onto her gums.

When I could think about anything at all, I thought that the simplest facts about what had happened would never be clear: when her illness commenced, when she was first aware of it, whether the manner in which she had struggled with it delayed or altered its course in any way; whether the manner in which we cared for her and fought to keep her aware of her surroundings helped to slow its passage through her brain; whether it was an illness of memory or an illness of selfhood. Simple explanations will not do. They fail to accord her the necessary respect.

We lit a fire every New Year's eve, up on the baulk of land that marked the beginning of the cherry orchard. I see her holding a glass of red wine in her hand, taking a sip, leaning on the rake, watching the flames. It is cold at our backs. The low hills are behind us in the dark. Our faces burn. My mother stares into the mauve heart of the fire.

More even than the fire, she loved the beauty of ashes, how everything – brambles, thorns, trees, leaves, creeper, grass, all the differentiation of things was reduced to one light grey substance which floated up and lodged in the cuts in the leather of her shoes. She loved ash, the way it guarded the heat of the last coal.

*

No one knows any more what should be said and unsaid, what should be respected and kept in silence. No one knows any more what proprieties should attend a person's dying. Certainly no proprieties were observed in the place where she died. Nurses at the end of their shift walked to and fro, smoking cigarettes. In the next bed, behind the green curtain, another patient coughed and sighed. There was even comedy of a sort, when a keen young intern entered the room and asked whether we thought some morphine might be appropriate, and my brother managed a dry, wise laugh and said, 'I think my mother has just died.'

I do not know whether it is an act of faithfulness to her or a betrayal of the dignity she never lost, to say that she had bitten her tongue, to say that there was blood flowing across her mouth and lips which my brother kept wiping away. I do not know whether I have the right to say, though I will do so, that her body was shaken with epileptic tremors and that she took enormous, terrifying breaths that went on and on until you could not believe she had the strength for them. I do not know whether, as we thought at the time, she could feel our hands on her forehead and cheek, or whether she had waited until we were both there to die.

I did not say 'I am here'. I did not say anything. Her mouth was open wide, as in those portraits by Francis Bacon of caged prisoners in their final extremity. I watched and listened to those terrifying, rattling, hoarse breaths, wondering at the strength remaining in her aged body and at the violence it still had to endure. I looked over at my brother as if he might know, as if he might understand whether she had the strength to continue. He was stroking her forehead, whispering soundlessly to her, attempting even at this moment to reach behind the veil and find her.

If you believe that she knew we were there, if you believe – I cannot be sure – that she understood what her sons needed at that instant, her eyes which had been shut and which, by being closed, made her seem completely out of our reach, suddenly opened. Blue-grey eyes, with a hint of yellow in the iris, eyes now beyond sight, staring up into the ceiling above her sons' heads, upwards, ever upwards, fixed like an exhausted swimmer on the shore. Then her eyes closed and she took the largest, most violent breath of all, and we watched and waited, stood and looked at each other, felt for her pulse and slowly, as seconds turned into minutes, realised that she would never breathe again.

There is only one reason to tell you this, to present the scene. It is to say that what happens can never be anticipated. What happens escapes anything you can ever say about it. What happens cannot be redeemed. It can never be anything other than what it is. We tell stories as if to refuse this truth, as if to say that we make our fate, rather than simply endure it. But in truth we make nothing. We live, and we cannot shape life. It is much too great for us, too great for any words. A writer must refuse to believe this, must believe there is nothing that cannot somehow be said. Yet there at last in her presence, in the unending unfolding of that silence, which still goes on, which I still expect to be broken by another drawing in of breath, I knew that all my words could only be in vain, and that all that I had feared and all that I had anticipated could only be lived – without their help or hers.

I KNEW A MAN once in my dormitory in college who graduated with a scholarship for Oxford. He left home, apparently landed in England, but never showed up at Oxford. After six weeks he sent a postcard home saying he was in Italy. Then nothing. This was in October. By Christmas, the police of three countries had abandoned their search for him. His parents placed an advertisement in the English and Italian papers telling him to show up at a café in Rome on a given date. Then they flew to Rome.

It's a cold January day. They sit in the café and the hours of a whole day tick interminably by. His mother is wearing dark glasses. So is his sister. His father keeps looking at his watch. They can't bear to look at each other. At the end of the day, the waiters start piling the chairs on the tables but the family is still there, waiting. Nobody wants to be the first to leave. The café has to close. The owner apologises but . . .

For the rest of their lives, his mother and father think: which do we prefer, dead or alive? Naturally, they prefer the former. The idea that their son is alive, somewhere, is much worse.

Some of his college friends thought he had lost his mind. Some thought he had been murdered. I cannot remember what opinion I held at the time. Now I think he simply wanted to vanish.

I appreciate that it costs me nothing to think this, unlike his parents or his sister, But I cannot resist the idea that he might be living in Rome or London, with a new name and a new existence, burdened perhaps with memories, yet also free of them in the most radical way which life allows. Of course it is a cruel thought. But then vanishing – like suicide – is an act of exceptional cruelty.

In the months after my mother's death, I kept thinking about this acquaintance. I began collecting instances of other disappearances, at first in the newspapers and then in literature.

I became obsessed with people vanishing, people walking out of their own lives. I began to write a book and I took this as a sign that I was slowly returning to life. The name I gave to the manuscript was

SELFLESSNESS

Through a freezing dawn in October 1910, an 82-year-old man, dressed like a peasant but with 39 rubles in his pocket, slipped away from his wife of 48 years, out of the house in which he had lived since childhood and was led by torchlight to a train bound for a secret destination. Abetted by his daughters and disciples, pursued by his wife and sons, he got as far as a provincial railway station, named Astapovo, 150 miles from home. There, in the stationmaster's house, Leo Tolstoy collapsed and died. Just before he lost consciousness, he said to his son Sergey, 'I cannot go to sleep. I am always composing. I write and it all links itself together like music.'

I do not imagine that he said this in a serene or happy whisper. Instead I hear something akin to the agonised desperation of an insomniac, bidding his mind to stop turning and deliver him up to sleep.

Astapovo and its meaning have always divided the biographers. Some maintain that Tolstoy was fleeing his family or his life of privilege. Others argue that he was running away in order to find a place to write.

I do not find these explanations convincing. He was not running away from his family, but from the person his family had made him. He wasn't running away to write. He was running away from being a writer.

He was running away from himself. This is not as contradictory or impossible an activity as you might suppose. If you can run away from your wife, your children, your house – and these are at least half of what makes you who you are – you can run away from yourself.

Imagine the volcanic force of the rage that propels an old man out of the house he has lived in all his life, out of the whole continuum of existence into a dawn flight. Perhaps only Tolstoy could have wished so violently to be other than Tolstoy. The self-consciousness required by the act of writing had made his own life unbearable.

Having read Tolstoy's letters and his diaries, I now realise how deeply he hated his own inordinate awareness of the world. He envied peasants because they were not divided from existence. They knew how to live and they knew how to die, and writing had not taught him how to do either. If he ran away to Astapovo, it was not to write but to lie down in a sheepskin coat and cease to exist, where no one could see him.

> But Pathe News was there. His wife was there, tapping at the window in tears. His disciples were there, taking down his dying words. Worst of all, he was there, conscious until the very last, seeing everything, feeling it all.

It was a strange experience to be obsessed by a piece of writing without understanding the least reason why. At some obvious level, I knew that I was filling the empty place in my day which had once been taken up in the nursing home. But I didn't think of what I was writing as a compensation for anything, or as a working out of some unresolved emotion. At every conscious level, I felt enormous relief that the long ordeal was over. I suddenly felt the strange joy of being utterly alone. I wrote feverishly, collecting more examples of people possessed of the desire to escape themselves, to elude the judging, wanting, hurting self: Kafka telling a woman he loved when he was dying of tuberculosis that he wished that instead of being a writer he had been a waiter, serving dinner on the beach in Tel Aviv; Rimbaud abandoning poetry and disappearing into the Horn of Africa to trade in slaves and guns. The Rimbaud whose letters contain the sentence: 'Je est un autre', I am Other; Harry Dean Stanton walking out into the desert in *Paris, Texas*; Malcolm Lowry, consuming oceanic quantities of drink in his cabin in Burrard Inlet, Vancouver, trying to finish *Under the Volcano*, a chronicle of the very process of self-destruction which created it. Was self-destruction the word? His drinking struck me as religious: to still the monitory consciousness, to silence the self, at the cost of his liver, at the cost of his sanity if need be, so that he might taste, while he lay in a heap, wetting himself, the fullness of pure being.

After a life of numbing rectitude, here I was identifying with drunks and visionaries. I wrote and wrote, never shaved, never went out, never answered the phone. I felt that at last I had learned how to live. Every day, I seemed to find another example of this longing to shed oneself.

> Consider Saint Augustine, not yet a saint, just a late-Roman sinner from Carthage, gifted with preternatural yearning for God and preternatural self-absorption (what a combination!) pounding his fists on his knees in a garden in Milan. It is possible, across the time that separates him from us, to hear him screaming: get me out of here! Out of this conflict, ferocious in its intensity, between his narcissism and his desire for beatitude, what was the result? The greatest record of selfhood in any language: *The Confessions.*
>
> Confessing what? That there is no escape from selfhood this side of death. There may be submission, mortification, penance, horsehair worn next to the skin, but none of these actually get a man out of here. None of them get you *gone.*

Only Divine Grace delivered Augustine from himself, into the realm of pure obedience: beyond wishing and wanting, hurting and desiring. But what about sinners, what about unbelievers? What about me? I spent two weeks reading Augustine's *Confessions*, in what strikes me now as a comic state of fury at my own lack of faith.

Her death had emptied me of any religious feeling I might once have had. There seemed only one thing that deserved awe and that was death itself.

It became obvious to me that I was one of those unfortunate people who happen to have a religious temperament without having a scintilla of religious belief. I found religious doctrines ridiculous, but felt the extremes of religious life drawing me like a magnet. The more I read, the more certain I became that the fasting, mortification and cleansing which all religions require of believers before they submit to god, expressed an idea I profoundly believed: that a self must be lost, before it can come to itself again.

Human beings are not naturally reconciled to the presence of a self within the body. Selfhood is not a fact of human nature which passes uncontested. Some people have always longed to be done with it, and religion has existed to cater for such a need. Whether this need can be satisfied or not is secondary. The fact that people even think of doing away with their selves, but not their existence, suggests that there may be some primal aspiration within us towards wishing to be done with the divide between self and existence, between us and the external world.

This longing for selflessness is *the* revolutionary counter-tradition to Western individualism. Alongside the long, noble history of Western self-consciousness, that infinitely elaborated project of self-knowledge and self-individuation that begins with Socrates, and carries on through Boethius, Montaigne, Pascal, Rousseau, Goethe, Nietzsche, right up to the apotheosis of modern selfhood, the modern rock star in all his or her extravagant and 'artistic' exhibitionism; alongside this mighty river of Western self-examination and self-advertisement, there exists the river of Lethe, the river of self-abandonment and self-transcendence, the pilgrimage highway of the drunks and the saints, all those who want nothing more than to throw their selves away. In order that they may simply BE.

Selflessness, in other words, is the counter tradition to Western individualism and its Me! Me! Me!

It is embarrassing to reread this manic treatise I wrote in those months when, though I was barely functioning at all, I imagined I was released, at last, from the cage of illness. Nevertheless it would be a mistake to throw all of this away. It is as revealing as one of those embarrassing, tilted, out-of-focus photographs taken at a party when you are drunk and have your arm round a stranger, and your eyes are red from the drink and from the explosion of the flash.

I, who had never been able to do without sleep, now wrote through the night, lying on my bed and then leaping up to run to my desk to add to the manuscript, which grew like a tumour. I even analysed my sleeplessness. It struck me that the reason sleep deprivation makes people psychotic is that human beings cannot stand any extended, uninterrupted period of consciousness of themselves. I didn't go out, didn't wash, looked out at the world through the dusty, then rain streaked windows of this apartment, and felt the lunatic awareness and exaltation of the sleep-deprived.

I thought ceaselessly of sex and all my agonisedly self-conscious attempts to achieve one second of honest oblivion. I began to see that my sexual life, meagre as it had been, had been a part of the same desperate struggle to get away, to escape my self, to take a holiday in someone else's body.

There was no sex now, with anyone. All I could do

was pore over remembered instants of oblivion, seeking to understand my hunger.

As for oblivion itself, I spent my days watching daytime TV. Only soaps. Only ads. Only they had the capacity to obliterate thought, to put the teeming brain to sleep. I never watched the news. News could make you think. The weather might start some unwelcome spasm of awareness. Even sports could start some manic episode of reflection. I remember a whole afternoon when, with the crazed concentration of a madman, I watched the final of the Virginia Slims Grand Slam from Coral Gables, Florida. Look at that young tennis player, I said to myself. Look at her young face, those eyes which target the incoming ball just like a marauding shark locking on to its prey. Not a pica-second of reflexivity comes between her and the ball. How I envied her selfless state of pure predation.

Look how gracefully she moves, how she springs into position for the next shot. I sat entranced, face inches from the screen. What is the word for this ruthless elegance? Grace. And what is grace but self-forgetting?

As my wife would say, taking my arms and folding me in upon herself, just dance. Just dance. And I never could . . . just . . . dance.

Of course I was depressed. I knew that. Of course I took medication, the last of my mother's green pills, what else? It was amazing how they slowed you down, how everything drained away to nothingness when you were on them, how you stared and stared, feeling nothing, not even aware of oblivion. I finished every one of them.

And I kept writing, now training these manic moments of self-awareness on depression itself. I wondered at my own strange exaltation, why I took such fierce pride in my state of mind, why I held on to my depression with both hands and could not be pried loose. In the midst of depression, I read books about it, I wrote about it, not to subdue and overcome it, but to go deeper, to visit its lower storeys, its caves and dungeons, the wettest, darkest places.

> Melanie Klein would have us think of depression as a longing for the lost oneness with the maternal breast. The individuation of adult life is thus haunted by a preconscious memory of a time when we had no selves at all. The self may not be natural, may not be naturally at home with itself; in depression, some rejection by the world, some success or failure, triggers a more essential disappointment with the project of individuation itself, in the form of longing for return to the beginning. The depressive is a kind of mystic and depression is a meditation on a lost paradise beyond the prison of selfhood.

I got this far in the manuscript and decided to send it to my brother. After a week I called him and asked him what he thought.

'I think Harry Dean Stanton should have kept on walking. It spoiled the picture when he stopped.'

'Seriously.'

'Seriously, you're trying to write yourself out of it.'

'We have nothing to fear but fear itself.'

'Spare me the Roosevelt. What do you want? Me to come up, or you to come down here for a while?'

'Neither, stay where you are.'

'I get the picture,' he said, believing that sarcasm would

do me good. 'All that distinguished company. Kafka, Rimbaud, Tolstoy,' he said.

'Get out of here,' I said.

'Well, you think about it your way and I'll think about it my way,' he replied. He said he was going for his morning jog, and I said, 'Good luck,' and he said, 'Look, we never close. Twenty-four-hour service. You call, and I'll be on the next plane. But do yourself a favour. Put that manuscript on the fire.'

The difference between us was that I thought there was some way I could think myself into welcoming the fate that I believed awaited me. He thought there was nothing he could do except study it scientifically, become acquainted with it as guerrilla commanders do, pitting cunning and knowledge against unequal odds.

Once, early in our marriage, I took my wife to Mexico, just the two of us for a week, and we came upon a chapel by the roadside – I can't remember where – and on coming out of the sunlight into the darkness of the building we were astonished to find a fresco of golden wings, flickering on the vaults above our heads. There was something frightening about the experience, as if we had surprised a flight of bats in the dark. Then we blinked and got our bearings and saw that they were, after all just images, water-damaged and ravaged by time.

Now I found myself thinking of my wife and that visit to Mexico, but mostly about angels and one angel in particular; the one who appears to Mary to bring her the news that she will bear a child. It struck me that the Annunciation, whatever else it was, can be seen as a fable about how human beings first react to the prospect of happiness.

Fear not.

That is the first thing the angel says to Mary. I bear you tidings of great joy. Joy and fear. Fear and joy, all mixed. We are so little accustomed to happiness, that any large prospect of it is terrifying. We fear even a happy fate. The angel understands. Fear not, he says.

Moe said to me,

'There is a subtle yet profound difference between giving up and letting go.'

Just let go. Look at me, Moe seems to say. I can't speak, I can't move, but by my soul I know what this life is for. I have had my visitation. So will you.

You are there, beside her easel, hunting for crabs among the rocks while she paints the Antigonish headland. And for the first time, the obscurity and uncertainty of memory dissipate and you see everything clearly: the blue band that ties back her hair, and her red shorts and her painted nails, and the little bristles of black hair on her shins, and the pursed expression on her lips as she chooses her colours, as she leans forward on her camp stool, the palette in her right hand, looking up at the headland, then at the canvas, applying the paint with small, precise strokes. She hums from time to time. She stops and reaches down for a plug on her beer, stuck between the rocks in a tidal pool. She smiles at you, and then looks back at the canvas. And the painting slowly acquires its shape, and the day declines in an arc, until you both feel the chill off the sea, and she packs up her easel into its compact carrying case, and she takes your hand and you clamber down from the rocks, holding a bucket full of crabs. The angel will deliver you back to where you always wanted to be, and he will leave you there, hand in hand on the shore. The angel takes you back to the beginning. When he escorts you across, to the other side of the gates of truth, you do not *lose* your memory. You *become* your memory – for the last time.

Suppose that she was beckoning for us to pass beyond the gates of truth. Imagine it as deliverance. Think of all the distinguished company: Kafka, Rimbaud, Tolstoy. My own mother. My very own Astapovo.

If I believed that, would I fear it then?

It took me many months, but I gradually understood, as I wrote more and more, what I was asking myself to believe. When I did, I abandoned 'Selflessness'. It was as if I had been like my Jack, when he was four, writing his name on the eraser board and then erasing it, over and over, experimenting with his own disappearance.

Now there was just my brother and me. I had hoped I would be back with my wife and children, but my wife said, in that quiet way of hers, 'I'm not as sentimental as you are.'

I said that I wasn't sentimental either. It wasn't the past, or what we had once been for each other, that made me want to get together again.

'So what is it?' she said, gently, as if she was genuinely curious to know the answer.

'I'm better,' I said. 'I've recovered.'

I knew she understood, but to her way of thinking, it was more honest to admit that something between us that had been broken and betrayed could never be put right again.

'It doesn't seem right to pretend,' she said, and I replied, 'Who's pretending?'

I said she was in her honourable, severe mode.

'It's more than pride,' she said. 'The truth is the way we were wasn't so terrific, and it's over.'

I said I respected her severe and honourable side, but she had a way of overdoing it. She laughed at that, but at the end of the day, she didn't budge. I had to settle for having dinner with her once a month and talking to her on the phone every few days. We got so that I could tell her most of what was on my mind, but not everything. She never fully trusted me again. She still wouldn't tell me anything about what had happened to her when we were apart.

At about this time, I came upon a small piece in a newspaper about the Adkins case.

Into the time capsule it goes, a frayed and yellow clipping from the *New York Times*.

> Dr Kevorkian's suicide machine consisted of three vials suspended over a metal box containing an electric motor. Once hooked up to the device, Mrs Adkins could press a button that first fed harmless saline solutions into her veins, then thiopental, which induced unconsciousness and then potassium chloride which caused her heart to stop.'
>
> Dr Kevorkian said he had asked several motel owners and funeral parlour owners for permission to use their sites, but all refused. So Mrs Adkins died on a cot in the back of Dr Kevorkian's rusty 1968 Volkswagen van. The retired pathologist called the police and reported the death as soon as the electrocardiograph he had attached to her showed no further heartbeat.
>
> He said Mrs Adkins was the first person to use the machine.
>
> Dr Kevorkian unveiled the device last year in a series of newspaper interviews around the country.

> Mrs Adkins, a former English teacher, who lived in Portland, Oregon, got in touch with Dr Kevorkian as a result of that publicity and flew to Michigan to meet him in a restaurant near his home two days before she died.
>
> Her husband, Ronald, and her three sons said she had made the decision to die nearly a year earlier. Although she was forgetting how to spell words or find the notes she needed to play the piano or flute, Mrs Adkins could still recognise her husband, play tennis and carry on a conversation at the time of her death.

Mrs Adkins seemed to me like a traveller alone on a wintry road at night, who feels the black branches over head and sees the blurred funnel of the road in her snow-dimmed lights. She feels the first signs of slippage under her wheels and decides to turn off the road. She kills the engine. She looks at her hands. They are white and still.

Philosophers are interested in Mrs Adkins. She is a case study in the limits of prospective judgement of alternative lives to one's own. The question they ask is whether Mrs Adkins can make a rational assessment of the life that is in store for her. I am convinced she can. She plays those notes on the flute and she knows that she has heard them played properly once. She still knows how they ought to sound, and she knows that she will never be able to make them sound that way again. She says to herself, either I play properly or I do not play at all.

Whatever decision you make – whether you chose as Mrs Adkins did or not – it is important to understand that it is a choice. You can choose to die, or you can choose that life beyond selfhood, the life beyond the gates of truth. How you choose, Moe taught me, depends on the value you place on self-consciousness. No one can decide that for you. You can choose life or you can choose consciousness, but as Mrs Adkins knew, the illness does not allow you both. If you do not act, as Mrs Adkins did, on the first signs of its presence within you, the illness will not even allow you the dignity of a choice.

It was a November afternoon when my brother and I buried my mother in the plot beside my father, in that sandy pebble-strewn earth, now tight and hard with frost. I told Fred Twomey from the funeral home that I felt like being left alone, and though he knew it was against the regulations, he tipped his hat and said he was sorry, he had known our parents all his life, and he and his people made their way back to the cars, leaving the two of us alone on the hillside with the light bleeding out of the sky.

I pushed some dirt into the hole with my foot and heard it thud on to the lid, then some more. I got down on my knees and began pushing it in with my hands, and then my brother joined in and between the two of us, on our knees in the dark, we managed to cover her over completely. When we stood up, out of breath, all I could see of my brother was the pale white disc of his face and the glistening patches of wet brown mud on the knees of his black suit.

It hadn't even occurred to me that we would pass the house on the way down from the cemetery. But we did pass it, and I turned back to watch its darkened windows pass out of sight, feeling nothing but the wetness of the earth on my knees and hands.

Suddenly my brother stopped, backed up and turned round into the driveway. We got out and I walked up the drive with a screwdriver in my hand and a torch beaming light off the pines my parents had planted. It was bitterly cold, the wheel marks down the driveway were rimmed with frost and our breath came in streams. A weak moon was rising above the trees.

I was wondering about the security the new owners were bound to have put in and my brother must have been thinking the same thing, because he laughed and said, out of nowhere, 'So what. The only thing that will happen is Fern Dunton will turn up in his squad car.' We had both been in school with Fern, and there was bound to be a way to explain to him what we were doing on our old place at night, even though, at that moment, we couldn't have explained it to ourselves.

Sure enough, the new owners had missed the fact that there was no catch on the left storm window by the kitchen door. Father allowed this omission from the high state of domestic order – all windows snug, all catches oiled and smooth, all sills painted – because we had to have some way to get into the place if we left our keys behind, and he wouldn't allow keys to be left where people usually leave keys, in the flowerbed by the door, or under the mat, or on the top of the doorframe. Seeing that catch missing in the light of the torch made me happier than I had been for a long time. The house had kept our secret. So it remained ours.

We didn't even have to break a pane, just pull back the storm window, slip the screwdriver down between the pane and the frame on the inside window and jemmy the catch back. I stood for a moment waiting for an alarm to sound, not caring whether it did or not. After a moment's silence, I got the window open and my brother followed me through it into the kitchen, tiptoing into the hall like two burglars in a cheap movie. Why tiptoe? No reason, just superstition and the dark.

In the kitchen there was a new German refrigerator with a cold blue light on the panel door, yet the table was still there, where we had left it, the table where I had sat with my mother and watched her trace a pattern with her finger, wondering how to tell her, when she knew already.

The new owners had taken up the green marbled linoleum my father had laid in the front hall, but I could still see him there on his knees, in his shorts, smelling of glue and sweat, stanley knife in his hand, slicing the corner pieces expertly and fitting them in with a tap of his fingers and then leaning back on his haunches when he was finished, silently observing all the tight, seamless joins.

In the living room, the rocking chair, the round scatter rug before the fireplace, the faded grey sofa, the bookcases full of Father's 1930s agronomy and chemistry textbooks and all of Mother's paperbacks, were gone, replaced with impersonal *House and Garden* stylishness. But the new sofa didn't matter, and the steel and glass coffee table didn't matter, and the plush pile beneath our feet didn't matter. What could not be changed was the disposition of space and the density of memory hovering about us in the dark. We stood side by side and stared out through the picture window at the garden. Something came into my mind.

'What was I saying when the car crashed?' I asked. 'I am saying something, and you are looking at me, but I don't know what it is.'

My brother took a moment. 'You were saying, over and over, "It was all my fault." '

'Why?'

'Father told you to stop bouncing in the back seat and you didn't. A minute later the accident happened. You thought everything that happened was all your fault. You still do. You never forgave yourself, though you can't remember a thing.' For the first time, I see and hear it as it really happened, from my father's curse, to my mother's scream, from the slow, tearing slide of the car, to the impact and the windscreen bursting and my father flung against the steering wheel, and my mother flung against the dashboard and my brother thrown up onto the hood. I hear the silence after impact, I see my motionless parents in the front seat and I see my brother pull himself back from the hood, turn with his hands covering his head and blood beginning to stream through them, and I hear myself say, over and over, it is all my fault. When those words are restored to me, I return back to where I am, in the sitting room of the farm we once owned, looking out at the gravel yard where our father died. My brother has turned and is looking at me oddly because I have begun to laugh and can't think of any way to explain why, except that it seems crazy that a grown man should have been oppressed for so long by something so long forgotten and so small.

I AM SITTING UP in a darkened room. My heart is pounding. I have no idea where I am. I am naked and I shouldn't be. I begin dressing hurriedly. I run round the room, bumping into a shoe, putting it on, bumping into a chair, finding some trousers perched there, putting them on, then a shirt, then some socks, and I am standing one leg in the air, with a sock in my hand, when a blinding light fills the room.

A woman is sitting up in bed opposite me, with her hand on the bedside light, looking at me with her hair across her face.

I haven't any idea why I am standing there with one shoe on and one shoe off, on one leg, holding a sock. I watch her closely. At any moment she may reach over and call the police. I have no idea who she is. I want to call out. I want to explain. But no words form in my throat.

Then she says, 'Come back to bed.' She is my wife. That was two weeks ago, and I tell it as she told it to me. Because I have no memory whatever of the scene. She says I had asked her if I could stay with her. The children were upstairs, asleep, and she said, 'Just this once.'

I came back to bed, lay on top of the covers and she stroked my forearm. But I knew I was slipping away from her. I could feel it happening, not wanting it to, and being helpless to stop it, just like an animal frozen in the headlights of an oncoming car.

Next morning I made an appointment with Dr L. He

knows my brother and we have been friends since high school. He arranged for the scans and the work-up. When I came back two weeks later, I sat down and suddenly it all seemed comic to be sitting there in his consulting room, going through the charade entitled, 'Getting the Bad News'. What part did the charade require me to play? Should I get up and shake Dr L.'s hand, as the writer Raymond Carver is supposed to have done when his doctor told him that he had inoperable cancer? Or was I supposed to sound like the great cinema gangster, who, as he re-buttons his shirt after the consultation, asks the doctor,

'Give it to me straight, Doc, how long have I got?'

So I began smiling, and I said, 'Help me. That gangster, in the films. What was his name?'

Dr L. must have believed that I had momentarily taken leave of my senses, because I then burst out with, 'Edward G. Robinson!' a little louder than I should have, as if to let Dr L. know that from here on I was going to contest every point, every rally.

He looked at me over the top of his bifocals. 'It's not what you expected.'

I asked him to read the report and not spare me the details. When he finished, I said, 'So it's too early to tell?' And he nodded and then he said, 'You almost look disappointed.'

I am in my efficiency apartment in front of the window overlooking the park. Through the trees I can see the nursing home and my mother's room, now dark. My window is open, and it is so late that the city is at last asleep. An owl in one of the trees in the park has begun to hoot and call. From far back in my childhood, comes the tolling bell of the freight trains. I can feel the cold linoleum under my feet in my bedroom at the farm and the hot stripes of the radiator down my pyjamas as I lean against it, watching the freights roll down the line to Chatham.

In the window's reflection, the frames of my half-glasses glint. My eyes have disappeared. My cheekbones catch the lamp glow. I have always had the feeling that I don't really know what I look like: what everyone else looks like, yes, but not me. But just now, beneath the flat surface of my own reflection, I see the shadows of two former faces hovering behind the outlines of my jaw, my eye and my forehead. Now at last, as I look at the night reflections in the glass, I see Mother, Father, the faces of the dead.

What was mine? What was the margin beyond inheritance? My wife believes that I wasted my life on these questions. I did not so much live my life as spend it wondering whether any of it was really mine. Just live, she always said, just live, as if it was the most natural thing in the world. And she did, with the grace of a born dancer. Now that the anaesthetic has taken hold, now that I feel so little, I can listen without pain as she says to me once more, looking up at the stars that night in August, 'What do you need to name them for?'

The reflection of my face in the window is superimposed upon the tracery of tree branches against the night sky. If you slice the grey matter very fine and put it under an electron microscope, the brain does look something like the dense pattern of the branches of a tree against the sky. But the analogy of brain to tree only misleads. Lop off a branch or two and it is good for the tree. Graze the grey matter with a scalpel and you'd take your wife for a hat and your hat for a wife.

Human identity is neurochemical. Human identity is measured in pica-litres. Infinitely small amounts of neurotransmitter fluid, microscopic levels of electrical charge make the difference between selfhood and loss.

Sanity is finely poised. Fate is measured in pica-litres. On the other hand, fate is beautiful. Feel the slow beating descent of its black wings.

I want to be done with metaphors. I want to see the thing itself. I want to see deep into the hippocampus, deep into the parietal and occipital, down into the brainstem itself to the places where the protein deposits are building up, millisecond by millisecond, forming plaques and tangles, shutting down the neurotransmitters, causing the circuits to close down, causing me to forget, more and more every day.

Nothing could be more beautiful than to see it happen: the molecular progress of your own dying. Lie back in the scanning room and watch your own neurons watching you, thinking your thoughts, being you, your own forgetting as digital squares of light on a video monitor. There, just there! My brother could point it out to me on the screen. That's where we would operate, if we only could.

Two thousand five hundred years of the Western fury to know would reach its climax right there: watching the molecular chemistry of your own demise on live TV. Talk about Know Thyself. It is just what human beings have always wanted: knowledge of ultimate things, the blur of time's fatal arrow as an image of flight on a monitor in a white room. Hey Doc, could you sharpen up the picture?

Think of Leonardo da Vinci's anatomical drawings of the foetus in the womb. Think of the eigthteenth century French anatomist who made wax models of women, which could be opened, so that the viscera stood revealed. This dream of the transparent body, of seeing inside yourself, has always been the fantastic underside of the official history of the self.

In the 1950s, when I was growing up, the Revell model company used to market two plastic models about three feet high, one called The Visible Man, the other The Visible Woman. Each had transparent plastic skin, beneath which you could see everything – kidneys, lungs, rib cages, arteries and the loose rope of all those bowels and intestines. You could take out each organ and learn to put them back in the right place. The models were scrupulously lifelike except in the sexual department. Remember, this was the 1950s, girls still wore girdles. The Visible Man was dedicated to the Socratic proposition: Know Thyself. But there was also that other injunction of the time: Keep Your Hands Away From There.

Imagine becoming your very own Visible Man. Lying there, seeing into the very heart of yourself.

Once, thirty years ago, when my left kidney failed, they put me on the operating table, under local anaesthetic, and wired me up to a television monitor, as the surgeon made a slight incision in my lower abdomen. I felt the pressure of the surgeon's forefinger and a painless sensation of flesh splitting apart beneath the blade. I lay wide awake, watching the television monitor as the surgeon proceeded to insert a tube into the incision and guide it up my aorta toward my defective kidney. I watched the walls of the artery pulsating, watched my own spine undulate when I shifted position. Then, with the dexterity of a car thief levering open a locked car door, he turned a corner in the aorta, arrived at the entrance to my kidney and pumped fluid down the tube. For several incredible instants, it was as though my blood had been brought to the boil.

When I opened my eyes, I looked again at the monitor and peered into my own body, as if through water, at the faint grey shadows which were my own vertebrae and my own lungs rising and falling like an anemone on the tide. I thought that everything I had ever believed about myself was wrong and that this was who I really was, just this surging pulse, this shape of bones, and the particular fate that had made my kidney fail. All this and on live TV! This was narcissism with a capital N. I had become the Visible Man.

I long to know, to be certain, to be face to face with the thing itself. I long to see the pathways of my own brain. My brother is right. No antidote to fear compares with knowledge.

The brew that is true is bubbling away in the chalice with the palace. Soon it will be approved and prescribed, to arrest the pathological cascade, and in the standard scientific manner, to transform a fate into a condition, to convert tragedy into something ordinary and unremarkable. As Kafka says, there is hope, but not for us. It will come too late for me.

I want to predict it in every particular. I want to imagine it as far as I can. What else is the examined life for? Is the manner in which I have come to understand it going to alter the way it takes me over? Is a disease observed altered by the attempt to observe it?

It is not as far-fetched a thought as it seems. Everybody goes through it differently. No one is ever just a case, a pure instance of the condition. A certain margin of individuality is allowed to each of us: one rubs his hands over his body, as if trying to reassure himself that he still exists; another one repeats all day the outlines of a general conspiracy against her; a third – my mother – stared softly out of the window at starlings drinking rainwater in the puddles on the roof of the Korean Baptist Church. Everyone finds their own path to extinction.

I read somewhere that Sir Walter Scott's last hours were spent in a state of pure graphomania, covering page after page with pure lines of meaningless writing, as fluid and as unbroken as the waves. He couldn't stop, no one could stop him, and he died with his head on the paper and his pen in his hands. Look over there, in the corner of the day room. Don't try to separate him from that greasy pile of scribbled papers. Leave him alone. Hour after hour, day after day, he covers the page, then recovers it, then writes up, then down, then across, then sideways, until each page is black with a million frenzied, meaningless words.

Does understanding *anything* make a difference, if there is nothing you can do to stop it happening? An excellent question, and one an entire life of introspection does not enable me to answer.

Will I hit her? Will I get up and run from the room when I see her coming? Half of me wants to hit her; the other half wants to say: I'm terribly sorry, he's not himself. Do come back tomorrow. I ask her forgiveness in advance. If such a thing is possible. I am getting maudlin. Stop being pathetic, as my dear wife, my one true love, would say.

She has phoned again. The answering machine distorts her voice, giving it an alien and disembodied edge. She says she has talked to Dr L. She says she is cooking dinner and do I want some. My children have called. My brother has called. Miranda has called. I can't figure out who must have told her. 'I just want you to know,' her soft voice begins and then the message tape runs out.

They all talk with the suspicion that I am listening. Their voices are extremely touching but I hear them as if they were coming from outer space.

I am holding in my hand a piece of shirt cardboard with one word written upon it. The line of the letters slopes down. Every one is agonisingly crooked and the places where the pen has come to rest are flecked with ink, so that the whole name has the appearance of being written, in the midst of a volcanic eruption shaking the ground round her. Yet, oblivious to the thunder of the explosion and the debris flying round, Mother laboriously completes my name. It is the last word she ever wrote.

Now here is a photograph of myself, at age six, in bare feet, in a pair of jeans held up with braces and a striped T-shirt. My hair is flying in the wind and I am standing on a rough planked dock with fishing vessels moored behind me. I cannot tell where I am, or who might have taken the picture. I stare artlessly out at my older self.

I wanted to pin this picture up on the bulletin board beside my mother's bed. I had already laid the pin in the centre of the top margin of the picture when I placed the photo in her hand. She held it there for a second and stared carefully at this image of a child who was once her son. Then with sudden, savage deliberation, she removed the pin and jabbed at the picture, puncturing both of my eyes.

There was not a shadow of a doubt as to what she intended. It had been a blinding. Now, of course, I understand. If you hold the picture up to the light, radiant illumination streams through the eyes. It is the light streaming from the terrain beyond the gates of truth.

What I know now, what I have learned from her, is that there are two forms of death, not one. In one form, everything which holds us in this world, everything we love, may remain precious until the last instant. Everything will stay as it is. Faces will mean what they have always meant to us. In this form of death, life holds all its beauty to the last second.

Then there is the form of dying in which everything familiar becomes strange, everything known becomes unknown, everything true becomes false, everything loved becomes indifferent, everything pitiful becomes pitiless, everything compassionate becomes as hard as a stone. This room will soon become a prison. The doors will be locked. I will try the handles. I will not be able to escape. The faces of my wife, my children and my brother will blur, decompose and then reform into the image of jailers. My own hands, my own face, my own thoughts will seem alien to me. The words I utter will make no sense, not even to me. I will be dying, but with my eyes open.

But I know that there is a life beyond this death, a time beyond this time. I know that at the very last moment, when everything I ever knew has been effaced from my mind, when pure vacancy has taken possession of me, then light of the purest whiteness will stream in through my eyes into the radiant and empty plain of my mind. Then I will be face to face at last with a pure and heartless reality beyond anything a living soul can possibly imagine.

The owl is calling from the trees. His hunt is about to begin. The moon hovers over the city and white light streams across the ivied floor of the park. I feel life calling me from this desk, I feel it bid me rise and walk out into the streets. The night is warm. My feet are bare and the sidewalks will be dry and warm under my toes. I will walk out to the end of the railway line. I will listen to the Chatham freights. I will feel the night breeze on my face. I will hear the road just beyond the orchard. I will see the lights of Alton and hear voices beckon. I will see the car lights, streaming through the night. No one will stop me now. The good Dr L. is mistaken. The scans are mistaken. The cells are too small to see. But I know. I feel them inside me. My fate has come to meet me. My voyage has begun.

ACKNOWLEDGEMENTS

The medical discussion of positron emission tomography and DNA gels owes much to conversation with Dr John Hardy and Dr Mike Mullin of the Middlesex Hospital, London.

I wish to acknowledge gratefully the permission of the family of Maurice des Mazes, of Kamloops, British Columbia, to quote from his private correspondence with me. I also wish to acknowledge my deep personal indebtedness to Maurice des Mazes and his family.

The quotation on the dedication page is taken from a passage by John Milton about his blindness, to be found in his 'Second Defence of the English People' in *John Milton* in The Oxford Authors Series, edited by Stephen Orgel and Jonathan Goldberg, Oxford University Press, 1990, p. 317.

The lyrics cited on p. 170 are from 'As Time Goes By', and are reproduced by permission of Redwood Music Ltd. Despite our best efforts, we have been unable to track down the copyright source of the lyrics quoted on pp. 13–14.

Passages from this work have previously appeared in the *New Republic*, the *Times Literary Supplement* and *The New York Times Book Review*.

This is a work of fiction. No resemblance to persons alive or dead is either stated or implied.